she told herself firmly. She couldn't possibly be attracted to this man. He was overbearing, churlish and definitely not her type. Even if he did have full, sensuous lips that— she banished the thought from her mind.

"I'm fine," she announced primly, smoothing down her suit and avoiding his eyes.

"You sure are," he drawled huskily, letting his eyes wander across parts of her body that she considered highly personal. "You're light as a feather, too, but a bit too skinny for my tastes. I like my women fat and sassy." He dropped an arm around her shoulders to give her a quick hug, and her pulse skittered.

"Fat and sassy!" she echoed in disbelief. He was getting just a bit too familiar with her. No wonder she was having difficulty controlling her emotions. She was only human, for goodness' sake!

Dear Reader,

Welcome to Silhouette. Experience the magic of the wonderful world where two people fall in love. Meet heroines who will make you cheer for their happiness, and heroes (be they the boy next door or a handsome, mysterious stranger) who will win your heart. Silhouette Romances reflect the magic of love—sweeping you away with books that will make you laugh and cry, heartwarming, poignant stories that will move you time and time again.

In the next few months, we're publishing romances by many of your all-time favorites, such as Diana Palmer, Brittany Young, Emilie Richards and Arlene James. Your response to these authors and other authors of Silhouette Romances has served as a touchstone for us, and we're pleased to bring you more books with Silhouette's distinctive medley of charm, wit and—above all—*romance*.

I hope you enjoy this book and the many stories to come. Experience the magic!

Sincerely,

Tara Hughes
Senior Editor
Silhouette Books

# SHARON DE VITA

# Lady and the Legend

Published by Silhouette Books New York

**America's Publisher of Contemporary Romance**

This book is dedicated with love to my sister,
Gloria Gunther O'Connor . . . a true Lady
and
In memory of my beloved brother
Kenneth Massie . . . a Legend

SILHOUETTE BOOKS
300 E. 42nd St., New York, N.Y. 10017



ISBN: 0-373-08498-6

First Silhouette Books printing April 1987



America's Publisher of Contemporary Romance

Printed in the U.S.A.

**Books by Sharon De Vita**

Silhouette Romance

*Heavenly Match* #475
*Lady and the Legend* #498

---

## *SHARON DE VITA*

decided around her thirtieth birthday that she wanted to produce something that didn't have to be walked or fed during the night. An eternal optimist who always believes in happy endings, she felt romances were the perfect vehicle for her creative energies. As a reader and a writer, she prefers stories that are fun and light-hearted, and tries to inject these qualities in the stories she writes. The mother of three, she has been happily married to her high school sweetheart for eighteen years.

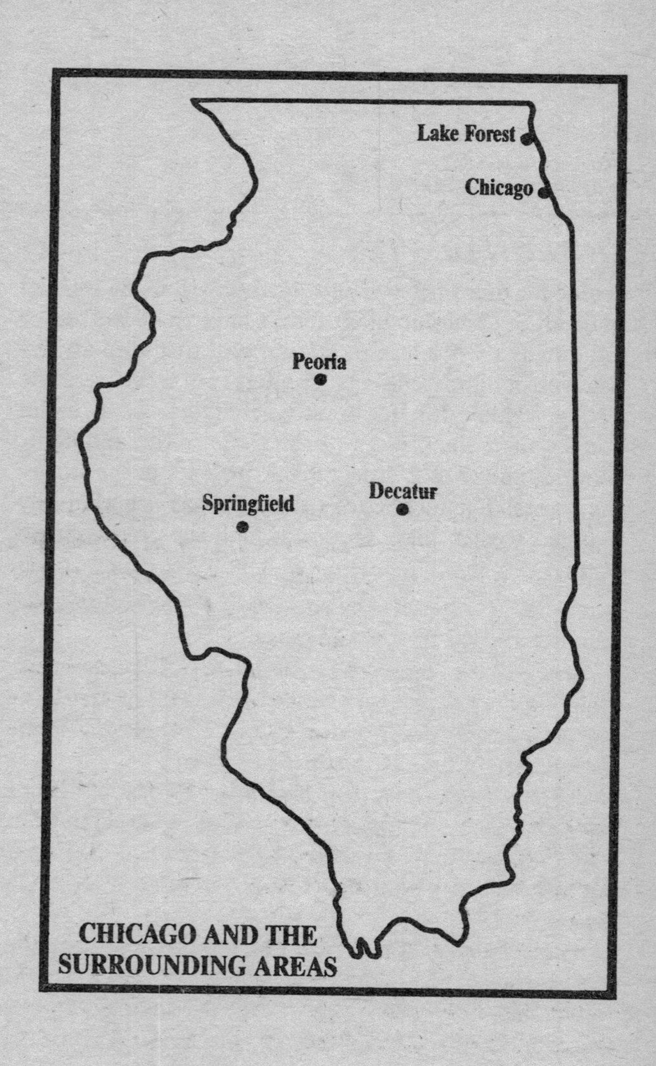
Lake Forest
Chicago
Peoria
Springfield
Decatur
CHICAGO AND THE SURROUNDING AREAS

# Chapter One

"Lady, you're about the last thing I need right now!" Gator McCallister's voice roared through the tunnel that led to the Chicago Cannons football field. The sound ricocheted off the cement walls and hammered against Victoria's genteel frame.

"I don't need my image improved," he growled, pushing his nose into her face until she blanched like a startled deer, "and I don't want some prissy dame following me around getting in my way!"

A bead of perspiration broke out above Victoria's lip and she fussily wiped it away. It was worse than she'd expected. Gator McCallister was as big as a mountain and about as pleasant as a warthog with dysentery!

"And another thing!" he roared. "You may be the new owner of this team, but I'm still the head coach. What I say goes. And right now," he bellowed, jamming his finger in her direction, "what goes is you!"

Anger sizzled her common sense. "Didn't your mother ever teach you not to point?" she yelled, poking her finger into his well-proportioned chest. "It's not polite! You don't need your image improved, Mr. McCallister! *What you need is a distemper shot!*"

Her eyes narrowed and he bit back a grin. She was Jake's granddaughter all right. Maybe she didn't resemble him in looks, she was much too prissy for that, but she sure as hell had Jake's spirit. And his temper, he thought wickedly. The old man would have been proud of her.

"Lady!" He inched closer to her until he was practically standing on her perfectly polished black-leather pumps. Victoria held her ground, refusing to back down. She would not be intimidated by his size or his anger.

Well, she amended, she'd try not to be intimidated, but Gator McCallister's temper was legendary, on and off the field. Good Lord, she thought wildly, eyeing the look on his face, what on earth had ever possessed her to speak to him like that? She swallowed hard. The man looked as if he was about to realign her facial structure!

He dropped his hand to her shoulder and a high-pitched scream fell from her trembling lips.

"Quit your yelping, lady, I'm not going to hurt you." He smiled at her startled expression. "You've sure got guts for such a dainty little thing."

"Mr. McCallister," she began stiffly.

"Gator," he returned pleasantly, all traces of bad humor suddenly gone from his voice and face.

"Excuse me?"

*"Gator,"* he repeated, his deep baritone voice skating along her nerve endings. "My friends call me Gator."

"In that case," she said primly, placing her hands on her hips and lifting her chin, "*I* shall call you Mr. McCallister."

"Will you now?" Rubbing a hand across his chin, he looked at her intently. His gaze swept over her, sliding from the top of the sleek blond hair caught neatly behind her head, to the wide blue eyes, fringed by long golden lashes, past the high, sculptured cheekbones, the small upturned nose, then charting a path across the long graceful curve of her neck.

Victoria's face grew warm and she stiffened when his eyes lingered just a moment too long on the curve of her breast before gliding down the rest of her slender length. Finally his visual journey ended and he brought his eyes back to her full mouth, which was now pursed in open annoyance.

"Would you care to see my teeth, Mr. McCallister?"

"No, darling, I've seen enough. You know, you're really not bad looking." Shoving his cap back farther on his head, he looked thoughtful for a moment. "I think you should get rid of those glasses, though, they make you look like a startled owl. And that suit." Shaking his head, he clucked sympathetically. "It's neat and pretty, but it's just too pale and severe. Pink just isn't your color. Now your legs are nice and shapely, but those round-toed shoes you have on make you look like an armadillo."

Victoria gasped. "How dare you!" she sputtered. "How dare you presume to—to— You expect *me* to take fashion advice from a man who wears a sweatshirt with more holes than material? And those pants! They could double as a checkerboard!" Narrowing her gaze, she gave him the full benefit of her icy blue eyes. "Any man who uses a rope to tie his shoes is in no position to give *me* fashion advice!"

"Whoa, there! Don't get yourself all worked up. I was just trying to be helpful." He gave her shoulder a friendly pat and his touch caused an unexpected warmth to surge through her.

"Helpful, Mr. McCallister?" she yelled, wrenching her shoulder free. "Helpful! I would sooner take fashion advice from a punk rocker. And another thing, I am *not* a little lady. Nor am I a dainty little thing! I would appreciate it if you would not refer to me in such a manner again." Victoria grabbed a handful of his shirt and glared up into his amused face. "Do you hear me?"

"Honey, I do believe the whole damn state heard you." He reached down and pried her fingers loose from his shirt. "Didn't your mother ever teach you not to grab strange men?" he asked, sweeping her hand to his mouth for the softest whisper of a kiss.

Victoria's breath fled. His mouth was soft compared to the rugged hardness of the rest of his body, and a ripple of awareness rolled over her. Taking a deep, labored breath she yanked her hand free, angry at the man and the sensations steamrollering over her.

"In the future, Mr. McCallister," she began, forcing her words to remain crisp and impersonal, "I would prefer it if you kept your hands to yourself. Unprivileged touching is a punishable offense in this state."

Much to her annoyance, he threw back his head and laughed. "Boy, that's sure a new name for it! If I recall, it was *you* who was doing the unprivileged touching by grabbing my sweatshirt.'' He rocked back on his heels and grinned down at her, causing her temper to flare anew.

Victoria mentally counted to ten. In French. She had been brought up to be a lady, she reminded herself crossly. A lady never raised her voice, lost her temper or resorted to fisticuffs, regardless of the circumstances.

''Mr. McCallister,'' she stated, with a good deal more patience than she felt. ''I—''

''The name's Gator.'' He smiled. ''What's yours?''

An exasperated sigh lifted her shoulders and she spaced her words carefully. ''What's my *what*?''

''What's your name. You know, what do your friends call you?'' One black brow rose playfully and his eyes twinkled. ''You do have friends, don't you?''

Victoria stiffened. Friends. The word brought back a momentary slash of pain, but she swallowed it back.

''Why, yes,'' she lied, forcing sweetness into her voice. ''I have friends. They call me Victoria. But you may call me Miss Fairchild.''

''It suits you,'' he returned pleasantly.

''Pardon me?''

He bent and spoke directly into her face, startling her. ''I said it suits you. Nice and prissy.'' Chuckling softly, Gator wound his arm around her neck and yanked her close. Caught off guard, Victoria froze, too stunned to speak.

The scent of the man tickled her senses. She would have expected him to smell a bit moldy, but he didn't. He smelled of soap and water, and something so totally male it caused her pulse to quicken.

"You're all right, Miss Victoria Fairchild," he said with a laugh, giving her neck another squeeze. "Yes, ma'am, you're all right. We're going to get along just fine."

Victoria stiffened. Get along? Get along! She didn't want to get along with this . . . person! She wanted to get rid of him! And now that she had finally met him, the sooner the better.

"Let go of me," she ordered through clenched teeth, struggling to break loose from his grasp. First he insulted her. Now he was trying to strangle her! The man was a barbarian.

"Coach, we're all waiting for you." A husky male voice echoed down the tunnel and Victoria stiffened. She could see a pair of dark-brown shoes, but little else, with her head hanging in the crook of Gator's arm and her face plastered against his massive chest. If the man didn't release her, lady or no lady, she was going to smack him!

"Come on, Tori," he said cheerfully, loosening his grip. "We're going to introduce you to the team." He dropped his hand to the middle of her back, nudging her forward.

"Victoria," she insisted, repeating her name slowly so that he would remember. "And it's not necessary for me to meet the team," she returned politely, struggling to keep up with his long-legged gait as he steered her down the tunnel. A menace, she thought in disgust. The man was a certified menace.

"Tori," he announced firmly, grabbing her elbow as he propelled her forward and out of the tunnel. "Tori the Terror, that's what I'm going to call you." He looked down at her and smiled, and she tried not to notice how handsome he was. "Listen, Tori the

Terror," he said softly, "you *have* to meet the team. You're the new owner." He gazed down at her and she wondered for a moment if he were deliberately egging her on.

She didn't have enough strength to try to figure it out. So Victoria simply nodded, realizing that for the moment he was the one in charge. She'd allow it for now, until she figured out how to handle him. But, sooner or later, he was going to have to learn that she was the one who was supposed to be in charge. And she *was* going to handle him—Victoria swallowed—she hoped.

"Now I want your promise that you're going to scare my players," Gator said with a serious face, as he helped her across the muddy field.

"I'm not going to scare your players," she snapped, as her high heels sank into the soft ground. Teetering precariously on the soggy field, Victoria lifted her skirt a bit to take wider steps.

"And pull your skirt down," he instructed under his breath. "My players are in training. I don't want them to see something they can't have!" He reached down and slapped the hem of her skirt free from her grasp.

"Will you stop that!" She came to an abrupt halt, put her hands on her hips and glared up at him, wishing she had never heard the name Gator McCallister.

"Stop what?" he inquired innocently, trying hard not to smile.

"Manhandling me!" she cried, glaring up at him. "I'm not used to it. And I don't like it."

His eyes slid downward, inching across the soft curve of her breasts until her face grew warm again.

"Tori," he said, bending to whisper in her ear, "maybe if you were you *would*." His sweet breath fanned her skin and another rush of warmth engulfed her as his meaning became clear.

"You—you—" She drew back and whacked him. Hard. The force of the motion threw her off balance. The soft mud gave way under the weight of her high heels and with a small, unladylike whimper, Victoria Louise Fairchild fell backward, landing on her delicate rear end in the mud.

Gator jammed his cap back with his thumb and clucked his tongue. "Tori, you really should do something about that temper of yours." He bent down and tried not to grin into her pinched face. "Now, I'll help you up, but, you've got to promise not to hit me anymore. You might hurt my feelings."

Hurt his feelings, indeed! She was going to hurt a lot more than his feelings when she got up!

"I don't need your help," she muttered, tugging down the hem of her skirt, which had risen to an unacceptable level. His eyes were moving up the creamy expanse of her leg and she blushed furiously. Did the man have no decency? A gentleman certainly would have looked away so as not to cause her any further embarrassment. Then she remembered: Gator McCallister was no gentlemen.

He heaved an exasperated sigh. "Do you want to let me help you up? Or do you want to sit here in the mud arguing with me some more?"

"Ladies," she announced, drawing the word out and giving it a great deal more emphasis than necessary, "do not argue."

"Tori," he said, "don't be stubborn, now. The team's waiting for me."

"Go away," she moaned, dropping her head as a wave of acute embarrassment swept over her. Never in her life had she had to deal with such a cantankerous, contrary human being. Why her? she wondered miserably. She never wanted to own a football team to begin with.

"I wouldn't feel right leaving you here like this, Tori. You're my new boss. It certainly wouldn't be proper."

Victoria's mouth fell open and she stared at him in stunned disbelief. "Mr McCallister," she hissed, giving her skirt a good tug downward. "I do not believe you would know the meaning of the word proper if it walked up and bit you on the... nose!"

Laughing softly, he reached down, grabbed her under the armpits and hauled her upright. The strength of his actions nearly pulled her out of her shoes. There was a loud round of applause from the other end of the field as Victoria struggled to get her balance.

Gator smiled then reached out to straighten her crooked glasses. "There you go, Tori, that's better."

"Better?" she repeated, indignation straightening her frame. "Better Mr. McCallister!" She deliberately said his name as if she'd just bitten into something terribly distasteful, not caring that neither her words nor her tone were the least bit ladylike. "You have yelled in my face, stepped on my shoes, wrenched my neck and nearly yanked my arms from their sockets!" She narrowed her gaze and gave him her haughtiest glare. "I doubt if I'll ever be better!"

He didn't seem the least bit disturbed by her anger. Frowning, he peered into her face. "You look all better to me, except for the little bit of mud on your skirt." He reached around and brushed at her backside. His big hands on such a delicate part of her anatomy caused a tingling sensation to race through the length of her.

"Take your hands off of me!" she cried, twisting out of his reach and trying to slap his hands away at the same time. She nearly lost her balance again.

"I was just trying to be helpful," he protested with an exaggerated pout that only fueled her growing fury.

Nostrils flaring, Tori pushed back the hair that had come loose and was now hanging in her face. "I'm not certain my body can stand much more of your help, Mr. McCallister," she said icily.

She pushed her glasses up higher on her nose then slid her hands along the lines of her silk skirt. The hem was crimped and wrinkled and her stockings were damp and caked with mud. A frustrated sigh shook her shoulders. Why hadn't she stayed in bed this morning?

"Tori?"

"What!" She didn't need to look at him to see his amusement. She could hear it in his voice.

"Are you always this cranky? Or are you just having a bad day?"

Bad day, indeed! She had a feeling any day that included Gator McCallister was going to be a bad day. Clenching her teeth, she gave him a look that should have dropped him on the spot.

"As a matter of fact, Mr. McCallister," she said coldly, her lips clenched into a tight, thin line, "it has turned out to be a rather bad day."

"I'm very sorry to hear that." He grinned and Victoria realized he wasn't in the least bit sorry. "Is there anything I can do to help?"

Help? Victoria clenched her teeth until her jaw hurt. "No, thank you," she replied, trying to be polite, but failing miserably. "You've done far too much already."

"Are you all right? You sound a little funny." Frowning, he peered down into her face again. Having him so close made her nervous. "Are you hurt somewhere?"

Lifting her chin, she deliberately ignored his amusement. "Your concern for my welfare is admirable. But, I assure you, I'm not hurt anywhere." She rubbed at her backside gingerly. The only thing hurt was her pride.

"Well then, Tori, I've got to go, the team's waiting for me. Why don't you go stand on the sidelines? I've got a new play to watch, but I'll be with you in a minute. Then we can talk." He grinned, obviously delighted at the prospect.

Somehow she didn't find the thought very reassuring. "Thank you," she said with forced politeness. "I think I will go stand by the sidelights."

"Sidelines," he corrected, then frowned. "Tori, how much do you know about football?"

Her chin went up. "Enough."

He smiled into her belligerent face. A smudge of dirt tipped her nose, and her chin was set at a defiant angle. The silky mass of blond hair had come loose and now hung limply alongside her face. She looked so vulnerable, he felt a tug at his heart.

"How much is enough?" His gaze locked on hers and for a moment her thoughts tangled. He had a way of looking at her with those dark, mysterious eyes that caused a knot to form in her stomach.

"Enough to get by," she assured him, struggling to keep her face blank.

His lips inched upward and his eyes danced merrily, much to her annoyance. "You don't know a damn thing about football, do you?"

"I do so," she protested, avoiding his gaze. A lady wasn't supposed to lie, but these were extenuating circumstances.

"Do not." He grinned.

"That's not true!" she cried, straightening her shoulders. "I know a great deal about football." About enough to fit on the head of a pin, with room to spare, but she wasn't about to admit such a thing to him.

He laughed heartily. "I knew it! You don't know nothing about the game."

"Anything," she corrected automatically.

"See, I told you."

"That's not what I meant and you know it," she accused, feeling a sudden urge to smack him again. The man was hopeless.

"Coach, we're ready." It was the same voice again. Although Victoria loathed people who rudely interrupted conversations, she would be forever grateful to the unknown stranger with the whistle around his neck and the clipboard in his hand who was advancing toward them as fast as his sturdy little legs would carry him.

"I'm coming," Gator called over his shoulder. "Since you know so much about football, Tori, would you like to come and watch this new play?" He was being just too polite for words.

"Another time, perhaps," she returned coolly. "I have some repairs to take care of." With as much dignity as she could muster, Victoria turned and limped to the sidelines, muttering crossly to herself.

It was hard to be dignified with your heels sinking into the ground, mud on your suit, hair hanging in your mouth and Gator McCallister in your life.

Digging in her black-leather bag, Victoria pulled out a white-lace monogrammed handkerchief and did the best she could to clean herself up.

Why on earth had she ever come down here this morning? she wondered miserably. Why had she thought it would be simple to inform the head coach of the Cannons that due to circumstances beyond her control she was going to be forced to sell the team?

In the six months since her grandfather had died, she had struggled vainly to hang onto the blasted ball club. But time had run out, and so had her money. She was dead broke. Busted. Victoria sighed. Even if she did manage to find someone to buy the team, the money from the sale would have to go to pay bills and back taxes. She'd be lucky if she had enough left for a new pair of hose.

There was no way she could continue to support an entire football team when she couldn't even support herself. She had no marketable skills, no hopes of employment. She didn't know how to do anything. She had never done anything, except play the perfect hostess for her grandfather and serve on numerous charitable committees. After raising thousands of dollars for charity, Victoria Louise Fairchild had found, after her grandfather's death, that the entire Fairchild fortune was gone and she was the one in need of charity.

There had been no warning. Her grandfather had never given any indication of money troubles, at least not to her. Not that he would have. Jake Fairchild had treated Victoria, his only grandchild, like a fragile flower to be protected from all of life's evils. No doubt he had hoped to recoup the family fortune before she'd ever had the need to know. But he had died before his luck changed and Victoria was left with nothing but the clothes on her back, a houseful of furniture and a second-rate football team that no one in their right mind would pay good money for.

Not that she cared about the money; it had never mattered to her anyway. What did matter was the fact that she was going to have to let down a lot of people who had counted on the Fairchild family. The idea of disappointing all those people, putting them out of jobs and perhaps even altering their lives, weighed heavily on her and kept her awake nights.

She didn't want to sell the team; she had to. Now all she had to do was convince one disagreeable mountain of man who called himself the head coach.

Victoria's head snapped up at loud commotion on the field. Her eyes found Gator. He was hard to miss. The man was tearing up and down the length of the field ranting and raving unrepeatables. Victoria shuddered. His voice was muffled by distance and the wind, but she didn't have to hear what he was saying to know he was upset about something. What surprised her was the respect he seemed to garner. Each and every player on the field was standing stock-still, hanging on to the man's every word. Somehow it didn't quite fit with his image. Hell-raisers rarely garnered respect. It was curious.

"Tori! Come on over and see this new play," Gator's voice boomed across the field. Determined to change the tone of their meeting, Victoria plastered a polite smile on her face and gingerly tiptoed across the soggy field.

They had gotten off on the wrong foot; now it was up to her to make amends and turn things around. She would be pleasant and gracious. Ladylike and professional, she reminded herself. And she'd handle him. She was going to take control of a desperate situation and correct it. The sooner the better. If she was going to have to work with this man for weeks, or perhaps months, she certainly couldn't afford to let her personal feelings get in the way. She was his boss, for goodness sake!

Somehow, Victoria didn't find the thought very comforting. She had a feeling Gator McCallister wasn't crazy about bosses, or authority. But, she had to hand it to him, he was apparently crazy about football. Or, she thought darkly, just plain crazy.

Satisfied she now had the situation under control, her spirits lifted. Pleasant and dignified, she repeated to herself as she watched the players hunch down near to the ground. Ladylike and professional.

She stopped in fascination as a group of men surged forward, knocking others backward.

Suddenly there was a heated cry from Gator and he raced toward some men who were lying around on the ground. Victoria increased her speed as best she could on her high heels and headed toward them. What was going on? she wondered, as she peered around the massive bulk of one of the players.

"Damn! Look at that shoulder! The bone's sticking clear out! I knew he wasn't ready to practice yet! He's going to be out for a few games with this injury." Gator's voice reverberated through Victoria.

With her mouth hanging open, she stared at the man on the ground as her lunch rose quickly from the confines of her belly. She tried to breathe, but the earth was spinning and somehow the air vanished before it reached her lungs. Victoria felt the world begin to spin crazily as her legs went out from under her. The last thing she heard was his voice.

"Boys! Someone catch the lady before she hits the ground again!"

## *Chapter Two*

Get back, boys!" Shoving a path through his players, Gator heaved an exasperated sigh before dropping to his knees beside Victoria's limp frame. Yanking his cap off, he began to fan her face.

His eyes anxiously went over her as a wave of remorse engulfed him. Maybe he shouldn't have been so rough to her. Hell, he was only teasing. Didn't she know that? He just couldn't resist. There was something about her prim and proper manner that begged to be teased.

She could have at least given him some warning, instead of marching in here today full of spit and vinegar and announcing she was going to improve his image and sell the team. He wasn't sure which bothered him more; her improving his image or selling the team.

Jamming his cap back on his head, he kneeled and scooped her up off the ground and cradled her against him. Lord, she was beautiful. Prissy, he thought with a mischievous grin, but beautiful.

Gator lifted his hand and tenderly brushed a tumble of hair off her forehead. His eyes slid from the tangled mass of gold, across the light brows and high cheekbones, finally settling on her soft mouth. A sudden impulse to brush his lips across hers startled him. She looked so lost, so vulnerable, it tugged his heart.

Sighing deeply, he adjusted her more comfortably in his arms. Like it or not, he was going to have to help her. He owed that much to Jake. But he didn't have to tell her that, he thought, biting back a wicked grin. Not yet, anyway.

Victoria stirred. Struggling through the murky depths of unconsciousness, she forced her eyes open, then swallowed hard, certain she had died and gone to . . . places unknown.

A tangled sea of metal and teeth stared down at her and Victoria closed her eyes again. This had to be a bad dream. A nightmare at best.

"Get back, boys, give the lady some air."

Even with her eyes closed, she'd recognize that voice anywhere. Stifling a groan, Victoria realized it wasn't a nightmare, it was reality.

She didn't move a muscle, nor did she breathe when she felt his fingers move against her face. His touch was gentle and the faint scent of him infiltrated her senses.

Victoria let her breath out slowly and tried to ignore the fact that she was lying flat on her back in the middle of a muddy football field, exposing Lord knows what to a group of strange men who looked like they ate raw rats for breakfast!

"Think we ought to loosen her clothing a bit, coach?" There was a round of good-natured laughter and Victoria stiffened.

Gator snapped his head around and glared at the man. "The show is over," he barked in a tone that brooked no argument. "Send the doc for Phil and head for the showers."

Victoria expelled a sigh of relief. She slowly forced her eyes open and was surprised to find Gator staring down at her intently, a worried look on his face.

"Thank you," she whispered, forcing herself to be polite and wondering why on earth she felt such a rush of gratitude toward this man when this whole miserable fiasco was his fault to begin with.

He was cradling her head gently, his hard, muscular body a soft protective pad against the cold, muddy field. A whiff of his after-shave delighted her dazed senses. Victoria tried to pretend it wasn't affecting her. But it was. She tried shifting her frame, but it only made her more aware of him.

Gator's tense features relaxed as he grinned down at her. "It's about time you came to," he grumbled, reaching out to stroke her face. Her skin reacted immediately to his touch. Vividly aware that he was just a few inches away, Victoria looked down.

The heat of his body warmed hers and she tried not to notice how close he was, but Gator McCallister was too big to ignore and Victoria squirmed again.

"Now stop wiggling, Tori," he ordered. "Take a minute to catch your breath." Feeling his gaze on her, Victoria inhaled deeply.

She didn't like the way her inner system reacted to him or to his eyes. It was unnerving and disquieting, not to mention ridiculous. She couldn't be having a physical reaction to him. She just couldn't be! He wasn't even her type.

"I thought you said you wouldn't scare my players?" he accused good-naturedly.

"Scare your players!" Victoria cried, stiffening in his arms.

"Yes, scare my players." He ignored her outburst and adjusted her more comfortably against him—from waist to shoulder her body knew the imprint of his. "My boys are very sensitive souls, Tori. I wish you could have seen them when you slid to the ground." Chuckling softly, he shook his head. "I thought a few of them were going to follow you. My boys aren't used to seeing a dainty little thing like you out cold on their playing field. It makes them a bit nervous."

"Makes them nervous!" she sputtered, pushing against his chest to release his hold. She couldn't take being so close to him; it caused stirrings inside that shook her senses.

Glaring at him, she tried to ignore the silent signals her body was sending to her mind. How dare he act as if everything was her fault! She'd had just about enough of this man for one day!

"Will you lie still until I'm certain you're all right?" His strength was no match for her in her disoriented state. Resigned to the fact that he was in control—again—Victoria gave in and relaxed against him. She knew immediately it was the wrong thing to do. Her heart thumped erratically and the blood seemed to pulse through her veins just a bit quicker. Her senses whirled, and she felt dangerously out of control.

Why was the man having such an impact on her? she wondered wildly. Victoria looked up at him. His face was so heart-stoppingly close her eyes did a slow inventory of his features. He was just an ordinary man, she reassured herself, with all the ordinary features. Well, she mentally corrected, you could hardly call the head of thick black hair ordinary. Seal-black curls glistened against the bright afternoon sunlight, falling with reckless abandon across his high, wide forehead. And those eyes, she thought hazily, were hardly ordinary; they were extraordinary. Large and dark, they dwarfed his other features, giving him a rugged, primitive look that took her breath away. A nose that she guessed had been redesigned by the best in the NFL shelved a full, sensual mouth that could by no stretch of the imagination be called ordinary. Victoria's eyes stopped abruptly. A full, sensual mouth, she thought dizzily, as her eyes slowly traced the lines of his mouth again. His lips, she thought distractedly, looked soft and warm, and terribly inviting.

"Do you think you're ready to get up now, Tori?" Gator asked gently, staring down into her eyes.

Feeling oddly breathless once again, Victoria didn't trust herself to speak. She nodded, hoping that her strange behavior was a result of the excitement of the day, and not the excitement of the man.

Without warning, Gator slid his other arm under her legs and hauled her up off the ground, holding her comfortably in his arms. She inhaled sharply. Wherever his body met hers, she felt warm and tingling, and her senses spiraled. She'd felt steadier when she was tramping around the soggy field in her high heels.

"Mr. McCallister," she cried, tugging her skirt down and trying to hang onto him at the same time. "Put me down! I'm perfectly capable of walking. Really."

Gator stopped abruptly and heaved a heavy sigh. She could feel his massive chest move against her breasts. She closed her eyes and tried not to notice.

"Tori, honey." He stared woefully down into her eyes. "I know you've had a bad day, but this hasn't exactly been a picnic for me, either. You've insulted me—"

"Insulted you!" She thumped his chest.

"Yes, insulted me," he repeated firmly, ignoring her squirming and fussing as he continued across the field. "Beat up on me. Scared my players half to death. And," he added, giving her a stern look, "you've disrupted my practice session. Now, I'm an amiable sort, but do you think you could let up on me just a bit?" His expression was so put upon that Victoria felt a wave of remorse for a moment, then it quickly vanished.

Perhaps she hadn't behaved in a very ladylike manner. But on the other hand, she reasoned, who could be ladylike with this man? If he wasn't stepping on her shoes or hauling her around, he was brushing at her backside or barking in her face. He'd had either his eyes or his hands on more parts of her body than she'd care to recall, and now—now—he had the unmitigated gall to tell her she'd been giving him a hard time!

Victoria swallowed back the spew of harsh words that threatened to fall from her lips. She was not going to let him goad her. Not anymore. She couldn't afford to. She needed this man; needed his cooperation. If he didn't allow her to improve his image, she'd never get anyone to buy the team. She was going to...handle him. Victoria swallowed hard. She hoped.

Determined to take a different approach, she lifted her gaze to his and looked at him curiously, wondering why he was giving her such a hard time. Unexpectedly, she found herself responding to the mystery in his eyes. Startled at the havoc he was wreaking on her usually cool mind, she laid her head on his chest and tried to regain her composure.

Perhaps it was just the stress of the past six months, she thought gloomily. Perhaps it had finally taken its toll. It had been six long months of trying to keep body and soul together. Six long months of struggling to borrow from Peter to pay Paul, knowing all the while that sooner or later her luck would run out and the only one left to pay would be the piper. But that was certainly no excuse to behave like a hapless shrew.

It was almost over. Now all she had left was the team. There was no choice in the matter. Aside from the fact that she knew absolutely nothing about football or the management end of the business, there was also the small detail of money, something she was sorely shy of right at the moment. From the looks of things to come, it wasn't a situation that was going to improve in the near future.

Determined to pull herself together again, Victoria tried to collect her thoughts, but found something was distracting her. A hint of Gator's after-shave mingled with his male scent. It wafted up from under the collar of his sweatshirt, tickling her senses and filling her with a strange feeling. Forgetting herself for a moment, Victoria buried her nose closer to him and inhaled deeply. Lord, he smelled good!

"Tori?" Gator's voice broke into her thoughts. "You look a little dazed. Are you sure you're all right? You didn't hurt yourself when you fell, did you?"

With a resigned sigh, she lifted her head. His brows were furrowed in concern and his eyes were gently searching her face. Her own eyes were level with his mouth and unconsciously she stared at him. His mouth, she thought distractedly, was so... How would it feel against... She blinked rapidly as the sensation took on life and grew vivid in her mind. Momentarily out of sorts, she lowered her gaze to the hollow of his throat, hoping for relief from the strange sensations that engulfed her. But the sight of a thatch of dark, curly hair peeking out atop his sweatshirt caused her pulse to race. What would it feel like to run her hands across... She sighed, trying to shake the thoughts from her mind. But they persisted. Up his throat... Across his mouth.

"Tori," he growled, startling her. "Are you sure you're all right? You're making me nervous. If you don't say something right now, I'm going to march you over to the doctor and let him have a look at you." He stopped walking abruptly and peered down into her face. She wasn't certain she could control her erratic emotions with him so close.

Angry with herself, she scrambled down from his arms, anxious to be on safe ground again. This was ridiculous, she told herself firmly. She couldn't possibly be attracted to this man. He was overbearing, churlish and definitely not her type. Even if he did smell wonderful. Even if he did have full, sensuous lips that— She banished the thought from her mind.

"I'm fine," she announced primly, smoothing down her suit and avoiding his eyes. "Just fine," she repeated more for her own peace of mind than his. Did fainting occasionally scramble one's brains? she wondered.

"You sure are," he drawled huskily, letting his eyes wander across parts of her body that she considered highly personal. "You're light as a feather, too, but a bit too skinny for my tastes. I like my women fat and sassy." He dropped an arm around her shoulder to give her a quick hug and her pulse skittered.

"Fat and sassy!" she echoed in disbelief as she stepped out from under his arm. He was getting just a bit too familiar with her body. No wonder she was having difficulty controlling her emotions. She was only human, for goodness sake!

Victoria realized she had to get them both back on track. She had to take control and let him know who was in charge. She was! she reminded herself crossly.

Drawing herself up regally, Victoria said, "Mr. McCallister, I came here this afternoon for a simple business meeting. Nothing about this afternoon has been either simple or businesslike. As your new boss—" She stopped abruptly. His shoulders were shaking with laughter, and the sound rumbled from deep in his throat. "What's so damn funny!"

Gator drew back and pretended to be shocked. "Ladies," he announced primly, shaking his finger at her, "do not cuss."

"I'll cuss if I want to," she snapped, giving her disheveled head an angry toss. She gritted her teeth as another burst of laughter rocked him.

"You know, you have the sassy part down real good. You're quite a sight when you get your dander up, Tori. Your eyes get all smoky and a little muscle along your cheek jumps. It's kind of cute." He reached out and traced the spot with his finger. Her nerves exploded—and so did her temper.

Seething with rage, Victoria stiffened her spine and drew a deep, shaky breath. "And do you know what you are, Mr. McCallister? You," she yelled, losing what was left of her composure, "are fired!"

Victoria spun on her heel and attempted to storm off, but all she could manage was an odd, jerky gait as her heels sank into the mush.

"Does this mean you're mad at me?" he called. His rich laughter drifted across the field, assaulting her ears and only further fueling her anger.

"Fired!" she bellowed over her shoulder, limping and stumbling as fast as she could to get away from him. "Fired! Finished! Finito!" she yelled, feeling an immense surge of satisfaction. And that, she thought with pleasure, is that!

"Victoria, what on earth happened to you?" James Bellows, head of the Fairchild household for over forty-five years, stared at her in disbelief. At seventy, age had lined his face and stooped his spine, but love and comfort for the woman he had raised oozed from every inch of his body. He had been mother and father, best friend and mentor for as long as she could remember. James was all she had left now. James was her family.

Her relationship with James had nothing to do with employee or employer, but everything to do with love and respect. James was the one person in the world she could count on, no matter what. And she had counted on him a lot, especially during the past six months.

Barely seven at the time of her parents' death, Victoria had come to live with her cool and aloof grandfather. Raising a child had never been part of Jake Fairchild's plan. He had turned the care of the bereft child over to the couple who ran his house. James and Lydia Bellows had stepped in to become Victoria's parental figures, lavishing love and devotion on the shy, retiring child. They had continued to run the Fairchild household with the practiced calm and peaceful air that her grandfather had come to expect. After Lydia died, James had stayed on, determined to see Victoria to adulthood.

James had wiped her tears, bandaged her scrapes and nursed her through every problem she had ever faced. It was James who'd refused to leave when her grandfather had died and her world had collapsed. James had been her tower of strength during every trial in her life.

After her grandfather's death, Victoria had been shocked to learn that not only had her grandfather lost his entire fortune, but in desperation, he had also dipped into James's pension plan, literally bankrupting it, in the hopes that he could recoup some of his losses.

Alas, it had been ill-fated. Her grandfather had died nearly penniless, after having lost not only all of his own money, but all of James's as well. All that had been left at the time of her grandfather's death was the house, the furniture and the Chicago Cannons football team.

"Victoria?"

Muttering crossly, Victoria limped into the house, waving one mutilated shoe in the air and slamming the front door with enough force to tear it from its antique hinges.

"Men!" she sputtered, not bothering to disguise her displeasure.

James chuckled softly and reached out a hand to steady her as she bent to remove her other shoe. "Looks like you've met the coach."

"The coach?" she muttered. "That man's not a coach. He's a—" She searched her vocabulary for a word bad enough to call Gator McCallister. "That man is a . . . barbarian," she announced finally, dropping her once perfectly polished shoe to the marble floor with a loud thud.

James's soft laughter echoed through the empty foyer and he patted her shoulder affectionately. "Now, don't be too hard on the coach. You know, your grandfather fought tooth and nail to get him for our team. Jake was convinced he could turn things around for us."

"Turn things around," she snapped, looking at her dirty suit in disgust. "The only thing that man is capable of is turning things upside down and inside out."

"From the looks of you, he did a pretty good job." His face twitched in merriment as he examined her.

"Good job, indeed!" She ran a hand through her hair in an effort to restore order to the tangled mess. "James, look at me! That man insulted me, yanked me out of the mud, yelled in my face—"

"Victoria, what were you doing in the mud?" James chuckled softly and Victoria heaved a weary sigh before leaning her head against his chest. His arms automatically went around her for comfort.

"You wouldn't believe me if I told you," she muttered into his shirt. At least he had the decency not to laugh.

"I know this might not be the right time, but—" He paused as her head snapped up. Victoria met his eyes and groaned softly. It was more bad news, she just knew it. She always could read James. More trouble. Just what she needed to cap off the day. As if Gator McCallister hadn't been enough.

She sighed wearily. "Out with it, James. What is it this time? The utilities threatening to cut off service again?" She cocked her head and waited.

He shook his bald head. "No. Can't say I've heard from them yet today."

Victoria tried again. "My car's about to be repossessed?"

He shook his head again, a sly smile curving his lips. "Not that I know of."

"The dog's sick," she burst out, throwing her arms up in in frustration.

James chuckled softly. "Now, Victoria, you know we don't have a dog."

"Well," she grumbled, "if we did, no doubt he'd be sick."

James smiled sympathetically. "I'm afraid it's much worse."

"Worse! James, after the past six months, how much worse can things get?"

Grimacing, he nodded his head toward the back of the house and an uneasy feeling began to snake along her spine.

"Out with it," she demanded with a sigh. "The suspense is killing me." She took a deep breath and steeled herself. James had a way of cushioning her against life's blows. If he thought whatever was about to befall them was bad, it was no doubt a disaster.

James drew himself up haughtily. "Mr. Malcolm is waiting for you in your grandfather's study. He's been here several hours."

"Roger is here?" she croaked. "In Grandfather's study?" Her shoulders drooped and she groaned. Just what she needed today, another contrary male. One who fancied himself Prince Charming, yet. "Why me?" she wondered aloud, rolling her eyes heavenward. "What does he want?"

"I'm afraid I haven't been privy to his intentions," James replied stiffly, and she bit back a smile. His face was screwed into a distasteful frown. His feelings for Roger Malcolm III were not exactly a state secret. "He arrived about three hours ago, insisting he wouldn't leave until he had a chance to speak with you. I tried to dissuade him, but you know how...persistent he can be. I fixed him a brandy. Several, in fact," he announced with a bit of censure.

Roger Malcolm wasn't persistent: he was a pain in the behind, and the last person she wanted to see right now. Particularly if he'd had a few drinks. Roger fancied that she was in love with him, not that she'd ever given him any reason for such summations. Why he imagined himself Prince Charming, one could only guess. Roger Malcolm III leaned more toward the side of the toad than the prince.

If she had known Roger was going to be waiting for her, she would have just as soon gone a few more rounds with Gator McCallister. Anything just so she wouldn't have to face Roger Malcolm III.

She let out a long, audible breath and tried to get a grip on her composure. What was done was done and there was nothing she could do about it now. Except go face Roger.

"Damn!" she muttered with heartfelt exasperation.

"Victoria!" James's dark eyes widened at her expletive and he chuckled softly. "I don't like to see you looking so discouraged. Things will work out, don't you worry." He gave her shoulder another pat.

"Don't worry," she muttered under her breath. What on earth did she have to worry about? She was dead broke, owed money to almost everyone, her car was about to be repossessed, the utilities were threatening to cut off her service and today she had the dismal misfortune of meeting a mountain of a man who had provoked her into behaving like a hooligan! To make the day complete, Roger was waiting to see her. Worry? What on earth did she have to worry about!

Her lips thinned and her nerves throbbed with fatigue, but she couldn't give up now. She might as well get it over with.

"I'll handle Roger," she announced with more conviction than she felt.

Without giving a thought to her disheveled appearance, Victoria marched barefoot across the marble floor, past the twin staircases that led to the upper-level suites and down the long, winding hall to her grandfather's study. She fully intended to make short work of Roger. She was in no mood for him or his antics. Pausing to smooth back her hair, she took a deep breath before sliding open the double doors to the study.

"Roger," she said sweetly. "How nice of you to drop by." Victoria painted a smile on her face and crossed the room to him. Quickly, her eyes took him in and she swallowed a moan. He'd been drinking, all right. His usually pallid complexion was now flushed. Two bright pink spots adorned his cheeks and his eyes sparkled with a brandied gleam. Blond hair that had been cut and styled by the best hair designers now fell with wild abandon across his high forehead.

For the first time, Victoria looked at Roger, really looked at him, and found to her surprise that she was mentally comparing him to another man. A man who was big and dark and totally cantankerous. A man who had loomed in her face and, she thought grudgingly, was now filling her thoughts. Roger Malcolm may be polite and privileged but, she realized, the man was a nerd. He was about as exciting as yesterday's oatmeal, and about as vibrant as day-old fish.

"Vicky, darling," he drawled in his best Ivy League voice. He weaved his way toward her and Victoria bit her lip to keep from screaming in frustration. It was going to be one of those days. She just knew it!

She accepted his kiss, turning her cheek at just the appropriate moment to receive his sloppy mouth.

"James said you wanted to see me?" Victoria moved across the room to stand in front of the stone fireplace, carefully putting a good distance between them.

"Yes darling." He waved his empty brandy snifter in the air and smiled weakly. She resisted the urge to lunge and grab the glass before he broke it. It was part of a complete set that no longer belonged to her. She had sold the set the day before to Mr. Androk's Antique Emporium. She couldn't afford to have Roger drop it. "I was wondering if you'd given any thought to my proposal."

She looked at him. What was he babbling about? She'd been too busy keeping her eyes on the glass he was waving around like a flag to listen to what he'd been saying.

"I'm sorry," she said sweetly. "What did you say?"

He sighed as if she'd lost her mental capabilities as well as her money. She knew, as far as Roger was concerned, they went hand in hand.

"Vicky, darling," he purred again. "I was wondering if you'd given any thought to my proposal?"

Her smile tightened and she resisted the urge to tell him just what she'd thought about his proposal. When she was Victoria Louise Fairchild, heir apparent to the Fairchild fortune, Roger had decided she would make fine marriage material. He'd said something about her good bones and genes, as if she would be enthralled with his compliment.

Not that she'd ever considered marrying the hapless self-centered bag of tweed. But she had never had the privilege of turning him down. When Roger had found out the Fairchild fortune was gone, and Victoria was no longer heir apparent to anything more than a pile of bills and a sagging football team, he had retracted his proposal. He had told her that there was no way someone like him could ever consider marrying beneath him.

She had rolled that term over in her mind more than once. When she had money, she was acceptable. Now that she was broke, she was suddenly unacceptable. It wasn't until that time that she'd realized her so-called friends were more interested in her bank account than in her as a person. They had abandoned her as quickly as rats a sinking ship.

When Roger had withdrawn his marriage proposal, Victoria had received the news with the graciousness of one who had been given a reprieve from the hangman.

Roger had then proceeded to offer a solution to her "current difficulties" as he referred to her financial problems. His offer was to buy the house out from under her. As he had told her at the time, "What on earth would someone in your circumstances do with a seventeen-room mansion on a prime piece of real estate in Lake Forest?"

When she had heard his suggestion, it took all of her self-control not to tell Roger what he could do with his proposal. Even she couldn't repeat such reprehensible thoughts. Not even to Roger Malcolm. Although the idea was becoming more appealing by the moment.

"Yes, Roger, I've given it some thought. Although your offer was extremely generous—" Victoria paused, almost choking on the lie "—I simply couldn't bear to part with the house." She made a sweeping gesture with her hand, and prayed he was too inebriated to notice how barren the room was.

When his gaze followed her hand, she knew with a sinking heart that he'd noticed. "Vicky, darling." His words set her blood simmering. "I really don't know quite how to say this—" He paused, and his blond brows furrowed in obvious dismay.

"Roger." She deliberately held on to her patience. "We've known each other much too long not to be completely honest. If you've got something to say, please say it." If the man didn't spit out what he wanted, and fast, she was going to turn him upside down and shake the words from him. She didn't have time for this nonsense.

Roger sighed heavily, obviously grieved by his thoughts. "Vicky, I realize that it's been difficult for you since you lost your grandfather." He paused and offered her a sympathetic smile.

What you mean, she thought angrily, is since I've lost my money. Naturally, someone like Roger would never be able to understand that she didn't give one twit about the money. It had never really meant anything to her anyway.

"And I feel for you," Roger went on, oblivious to her growing anger. "I really do. But you must be practical. What on earth are you going to do with the house? You certainly can't afford to keep it, not in your current circumstances. Let me help you out. Sell me the place."

Her sweet smile hid her venomous thoughts. Help her out, indeed. The only person Roger was concerned with helping was Roger. She'd known him too long not to know he was up to something. His sudden interest in this house was just too coincidental.

Victoria moved around the empty room, struggling to compose herself. "Roger, I appreciate your concern, but I really couldn't allow you to help me. I simply couldn't impose on your generosity." She forced her mouth to smile, but her teeth were clenched so tightly her jaw hurt.

"Vicky, darling, I insist. I'll be happy to write you out a check right now. Name your price, within reason, of course," he added, with a wicked chuckle.

"Why this house, Roger? With your money, certainly you can afford to buy any home you choose." Victoria turned a sharp eye on him and watched his face turn bright pink. She was right, he was up to something.

"Well, to be perfectly honest—" he paused to drain the last few drops in his glass "—I promised it to Bonni as a wedding present." He grinned sheepishly and Victoria's perfectly arched brows rose.

Roger was marrying Bonni? She nearly choked on a chuckle. Roger and Bonni! She couldn't think of two people who deserved each other more. Victoria had always felt Bonni's ship was missing a few sails. If the poor girl had agreed to marry Roger, Victoria was certain of it.

"You promised Bonni this house?" she asked, spacing her words carefully. If Roger wanted to marry Bonni, that was his business. But when he started promising Victoria's house to someone, that was another story!

"Why, yes, darling," he went on, totally oblivious to the danger signals in her eyes. "Bonni's just absolutely in love with the place. Thinks it's absolutely top drawer. I was sure you wouldn't mind. I thought you'd be grateful to get rid of it."

At the moment, she would have been grateful to get rid of him. Permanently.

"Roger," she said briskly, not caring to discuss the matter any further. "I'm sorry, this house is not for sale. Not to you or to Bonni. You'll have to find something else to give her for a wedding present."

To no one would she admit the house didn't even belong to her. It belonged to James. At the time of her grandfather's death, Victoria received the Cannons and all the furniture, but the house and property were left to James, as repayment for the money her grandfather had "borrowed" from James's pension fund. But she'd die before she told Roger or anyone else that. James had offered to sell the house numerous times over the past six months, but Victoria wouldn't let him. The house was his, and he was going to keep it and enjoy it. After all his years with the Fairchild family, it was the least he deserved. As it was, he had thrown in what was left of his meager savings to help her along the past few months. She owed him so much, there was no way she was going to let the man sell the house to support her, too.

Roger weaved his way closer and for the first time Victoria noted the unnatural gleam in his eye. She backed up until her spine was pressed against the cool stone of the fireplace.

"Darling, I know you must have been hurt when I broke it off with you. And granted, Bonni isn't you, but she's sweet and I'm sure we'll make a fine marriage. But that's no reason why we can't continue..." He searched for the right word. "Our... relationship." Smiling, he went on without noticing her shock. "Once Bonni and I move in here, I can set you up in a little apartment in town. Just big enough for the two of us. It will be wonderful, darling. Our own little love nest." His eyes sparkled and his breathing grew shallow.

Victoria gaped at him. Love nest? The only kind of nest Roger needed was a padded one, and if he continued in this vein, she was going to see that he got one!

Roger took her silence as agreement and lunged toward her. Victoria tried to step back but there was no place to go; the fireplace was at her back. Roger's voice dropped to a slurred whisper as he murmured her name. He leaned his thin body against hers, pinning her to the fireplace. He bent his head to nuzzle her neck and Victoria nearly reeled from the fumes of his breath.

"Let go of me, please!" She twisted her face to avoid his searching mouth.

"Vicky, darling," he cried passionately, planting his mouth firmly on hers.

"Roger Malcolm, behave yourself!" She twisted her head away as the taste of brandy assaulted her mouth. Lifting her hands to his chest, she gave him a good shove.

"I always knew there was a hot-blooded woman inside that cool exterior," he whispered huskily, attempting to find her mouth again. Victoria heaved an exasperated sigh. Why her? Was it her misfortune to meet every contrary male in the world today?

"Roger Malcolm, if you don't let go of me this instant, I won't be responsible for my actions!"

"Yes, darling, I know just how you feel," he said, his breathing ragged and uneven. "Let yourself go, darling. Just let yourself go!" Roger's hand began roaming from the curve of her waist upward.

"Roger!" she cried, trying not to laugh at his clumsy attempts at passion. "Stop this right now! Or—or I'll tell your mother," she threatened, trying to struggle free. Her attempts only fanned his desire and Roger clung tighter to her, slobbering against her neck.

"Roger!" she shrieked, trying to give him a shove.

"What the hell s going on here?" a deep baritone voice bellowed from the doorway.

Victoria's stunned gaze flew to the doorway. Gator! What was he doing here? She didn't know whether to cry or laugh, she was so glad to see him. An hour ago, she would never have thought such a feeling was possible. Right now she didn't care why he was here. She was just grateful he was.

Roger's glazed eyes slid to the man looming menacingly in the doorway. He didn't have enough sense to recognize danger when he saw it. The look on Gator's face would have been enough to frighten any reasonable person.

"Go away," Roger snapped crankily, obviously disturbed by the sudden interruption. Having dismissed Gator, he turned his attention back to Victoria, who gave him another shove.

"Gator!" she called helplessly, as Roger's mouth searched for hers. She wasn't even aware she had cried out his name until she watched him storm the length of the room.

Cursing softly under his breath, Gator grabbed Roger by the scruff of his collar and hoisted him bodily off the floor.

Stunned, Roger's eyes rounded and he turned to stare blankly at her. "Vicky! Who is this person?" he demanded, his lashes flapping furiously.

Gator scowled and gave Roger a little shake. "My name's Gator," he ground out, glaring into the smaller man's face.

"As in a . . . alligator?" Roger whispered hoarsely. His feet dangled off the ground and he was in danger of losing one of his tasseled loafers.

"Do you have a problem with that?" Gator barked, pushing his face into Roger's until Victoria was certain the smaller man was going to faint. Roger's Adam's apple bobbed furiously and his lashes were going up and down a mile a minute, as if he couldn't believe his eyes.

Victoria couldn't help it, she started to giggle. Obviously Roger wasn't fond of alligators, either the human or the reptile kind. She had to admit though, she was feeling a growing attachment to them herself.

"P-problem?" Roger squeaked. "N-no," he sputtered, waving his hands in the air. "N-no problem."

"Good." Gator turned to Victoria and flashed her a quick smile. She could see the amusement in his eyes. She couldn't help it, she was charmed. "Is this man a friend of yours?" he asked.

Before she could answer Roger spoke up. "Friend? No, I . . . I—" He stopped abruptly and gave Victoria a terrified look.

"You were just leaving?" Gator supplied helpfully, giving Victoria a wink over the top of Roger's head.

"Yes. Yes," Roger confirmed, bobbing his head in a frantic motion. "I was just leaving. Right, Vicky?"

If he was hoping for her to bail him out, he had a long wait, she thought, trying to swallow back the laughter that was bubbling inside of her.

"Yes, I was just leaving," Roger repeated.

"I thought so," Gator announced, marching across the room with Roger in tow. "James?" Gator bellowed. "Open the door. I've got some trash to throw out!"

# *Chapter Three*

The moment Gator marched through the door, Victoria burst into uncontrollable laughter, wilting to the floor like week-old roses. There was a definite advantage to being churlish and overbearing, she decided, wiping a tear from her eye. Too bad James hadn't been around. No doubt he would have enjoyed seeing Roger cut down a few pegs. She had to admit, she kind of enjoyed it herself.

"Did he hurt you?" Gator barked from the doorway, causing her to jump. He stormed across the room and stared down at her. The look on his face was so menacing, Victoria started laughing again. She couldn't help but wonder how Roger would react if he ever saw Gator in full bloom. She wiped her teary eyes as she imagined the scene. Poor Roger would probably never recover.

"Are you crying?" Gator asked as his eyes darkened ominously. "He did hurt you, didn't he?" Before she could stop him he spun on his heels and marched toward the door. "When I get my hands on that—"

"Gator, wait." Victoria scrambled up and tore after him. She grabbed his arm just as he was about to stomp through the doorway. "He didn't hurt me, Gator," she said. "I'm not crying. I'm laughing."

"Laughing?" Tipping her chin upward, Gator examined her more closely. His touch was deliberately gentle and caused her pulse to skid. He had showered and changed, she noticed. His dark, curly hair was still damp and fell recklessly around his face. It had a tousled look, as if he had combed it with nothing more than his fingers. She noted the streaks of silver touching his temples. The sweatshirt was gone, replaced by a navy-blue shirt that caressed his wide shoulders. The collar was left unbuttoned, the long sleeves rolled up to reveal strong, muscled forearms dusted with dark, curly hair. Faded jeans that were just a breath away from being indecently tight hugged his lean hips and long legs. The gym shoes were gone, replaced by snakeskin boots that only added to his immense height. Still barefoot, Victoria barely reached his shoulders. His new attire added a different dimension to him. Gator no longer looked like a churlish, overbearing football coach. What he looked like, she thought, trying to get her mind back on track, was a devastatingly handsome man. For some reason, it bothered her. She didn't feel quite so much in control with him like this. He now seemed more normal and very, very appealing. He was having a definite effect on her. Even if he wasn't her type.

"Are you sure he didn't hurt you?" His voice was soft and soothing and Victoria merely nodded.

Roger hadn't hurt her, at least not physically. The only thing he had hurt was her pride. But, in the state Gator was in, she wasn't about to admit any such thing to him.

"Tori, honey, who the hell was that guy and what did he want?"

"His name is Roger Malcolm III." Victoria withdrew her hand from his arm, hoping it would be easier to put her thoughts together if she weren't touching him.

"You mean to tell me there's two more like him at home?" Gator groaned and jammed his hand through his hair. "What did he want?"

Why did she have the feeling her answer was not going to please him? She watched his face carefully, realizing she couldn't tear her eyes away even if she wanted to. "Roger wanted my house and my body, but not necessarily in that order."

"What!" His frown deepened to a scowl that brought another smile to her lips.

"My house and my body," she repeated, not bothering to suppress the chuckle that broke loose. He looked clearly appalled, and she had to admit it was fun watching him come unglued. Before, she would have sworn that nothing could faze him. Now she knew differently. She had to admit it was charming.

Suddenly he smiled wickedly. His eyes inched over her frame, bringing a warm glow to her face. "I can understand him wanting your body, honey. But what the hell does he want your house for? Can't he buy one of his own?"

"He can afford to buy any house he wants," Victoria explained with a small laugh. "But it seems he wants this one."

"Why?" Gator glanced around the room in obvious confusion.

"He promised it to Bonni."

"Is that supposed to make sense? Who the hell is Bonni and why did he promise her your house?"

"It's a long story." She shrugged her shoulders. "Bonni is the woman Roger's going to marry and she likes this house."

"You mean he actually convinced someone to marry him?" His deep voice was incredulous and Victoria laughed again.

"Yes. And he was trying to convince me to be his new playmate. He offered to set me up in a little love nest."

"Playmate! If that guy wants a playmate, I'll give him a playmate. The one I've got in mind is six-foot-six and about two hundred and seventy pounds. I guarantee he'll give Roger an afternoon he won't forget!"

Gator's sudden protective attitude was surprising and Victoria found it a bit odd, considering what he'd put her through earlier that day. But she found his presence reassuring, a fact that she would have vehemently denied just a few hours ago.

She bit back a smile. Gator McCallister was a fraud. A big fake. Oh, he was big and he barked and made a lot of loud noises, but she had a feeling he was about as dangerous as a newborn puppy. And probably about as frisky. He was blustering and fuming so much she was beginning to enjoy herself.

"I guess that's the way you folks do things," he said sadly, shaking his head. "You promise houses that don't belong to you and make indecent proposals to women you're not married to."

*"We folks!"* she blurted, her eyes wide. "What do you mean, 'we folks'?" She didn't like the idea of being put in the same category as Roger and Bonni. But then again, she had to admit, she could understand Gator automatically assuming she was just like them. Outwardly, at least, she must seem as if she were just like them. But she wasn't. She wasn't anything like Roger or Bonni, with or without money.

"Now, Tori, don't tell me you're mad at me again?" Smiling gently, he reached out and smoothed back a strand of her hair. His fingers traced the curve of her earlobe, exploding her senses with delight.

"Gator," she asked breathlessly. "What are you doing here?"

"Aren't you glad to see me?" He grinned sheepishly and she tried not to smile.

"To tell you the truth," she admitted, "I've never been so glad to see anyone in my life. Roger isn't usually so hard to handle, but he had a few drinks and..." Her voice trailed off. Gator's closeness was disrupting her thought process. "Thank you," she murmured, suddenly feeling all addled. She was struck by how vulnerable she felt in his presence. It left her feeling oddly uncomfortable. Perhaps it was just the excitement of the day, she reasoned. Or, an inner voice corrected, perhaps it was the excitement of the man.

"You're welcome." He seemed content to stand there and stare at her, but his unwavering gaze made her increasingly uncomfortable.

"Gator, why are you here?" she blurted out. "Was there something you wanted?" The moment the words were out, she knew it was the wrong thing to say. His face split into a wide grin and he chuckled softly.

"That depends, Tori. What are you offering?"

"Nothing." She laughed. "Just a simple thank-you. And an apology."

He frowned at her. "What have you got to apologize for?"

Victoria sighed and raked a hand through her hair. "Well, if I remember correctly, you said I beat up on you, insulted you, scared your players and disrupted your practice. Have I covered everything?"

"Just about," he agreed, nodding. "But you don't have to apologize. I was just having some fun with you." There was mischief in his eyes.

Victoria's mouth fell open. "You mean you deliberately—"

He raised his hand to silence her. "Now don't get mad at me again. You just apologized, remember? How about a truce?" His grin was so appealing she found her resistance melting.

"All right, a truce," she agreed, then stopped short. "But you still haven't told me what you're doing here."

"I thought we'd better talk." He stepped around her to survey the room. "What happened to all the furniture that used to be in here?" He strolled around the nearly empty room, the heels of his boots clicking softly on the oak flooring. "The last time I came to see Jake there was a big desk here and a piano in that corner."

Victoria's eyes followed the path he was tracing, past the empty corner where the Van Cordtland cupboard had sat, past the fireplace where the twin leather couches had nestled, past the expansive nook where the baby grand had perched for nearly three generations. It was all gone now. The room was nearly bare.

The only reminder a slight outline on the oak flooring where the Aubusson carpet had once been.

"I sold it," she informed him simply, lifting her eyes to his. One dark brow rose but he said nothing as he continued walking slowly around the room until he was standing in front of her again.

"Everything?"

She nodded. "Everything."

"Didn't you like it?" He looked down at her and Victoria blinked.

There was something about his eyes, she decided, that seemed to muddle her brain. Or was it his closeness, she wondered distractedly, unable to pull her gaze from his. She found her eyes wandering to his mouth again and felt her equilibrium nosedive.

"Didn't I like what?" she whispered, struggling to pick up the thread of their conversation.

"The furniture." Lifting a finger, he began to stroke her chin. It was an innocent gesture, but the masculine scent of him caused her senses to whirl. She longed to back away from his touch, aware that his nearness was a great deal more than she could handle at the moment. Perhaps at any moment. But she couldn't seem to move.

"I . . . I liked it," she whispered softly.

"Then why did you sell it?" He was looking at her so intently, she lowered her eyes. He reached out and cupped her chin, forcing her head upward. The intensity of his gaze caused her heart to thud recklessly against her breast. She was silent as she concentrated on the touch of his fingers and the look in his eyes.

"Why?" he persisted, stroking her skin tenderly. For such a big man, he was decidedly gentle. She had the irresistible urge to nestle her cheek against his hand

and pour out the whole miserable story. What possible difference could it make now? she wondered dismally. What was done was done, and she certainly couldn't change it now.

"I needed the money." Swallowing the last remnants of her pride, Victoria wondered why on earth she was telling him all this.

He cast a quick glance around the room and whistled softly. "I imagine it must take a lot to keep up a house like this."

She detected just a hint of censure in his tone and reacted immediately. He had no idea what she'd been through these past six months. No idea how she had struggled and fought until there was almost no fight left in her anymore. And it had nothing whatsoever to do with keeping up the house. It had to do with survival. But she wasn't about to admit such a thing, not to him, not to anyone. She still had some pride.

"I didn't sell the furniture to keep up the house," she defended hotly, struggling to control her temper. She didn't know why it was so important to her but she didn't want him thinking ill of her. She didn't want him to think that she had sold everything simply to keep the house and keep up appearances. Nothing could be further from the truth.

"Then why did you sell it?"

"Why are you here?"

"I already told you," he returned pleasantly. "I guess you just weren't listening to me. I think we should talk."

"There's nothing to talk about. I believe we both said everything we had to earlier today. I appreciate you coming to my rescue but—"

He dropped his hands to her shoulders and gave her a little squeeze. "Tori, you're mad again." He tightened his fingers on her shoulders to keep her in place as she tried to duck out from under his hold.

"I just want to help," he continued. He smiled and his eyes seemed to draw her. She knew it was dangerous, but she couldn't pull her gaze from his. There was something in his eyes, some emotion she couldn't identify. Maybe he really did want to help, but there was nothing he could do. Nothing anyone could do.

"I appreciate the offer," she said politely, dropping her eyes to the middle of his chest. "But there's nothing you can do. Besides," she couldn't resist adding, "I thought I fired you."

"You can't fire me, Tori," he said, with just a bit of humor.

Her head snapped up. "I can and I did. Maybe you weren't listening."

"Oh, I was listening, all right. But you still can't fire me." He grinned broadly into her confused face.

Victoria tensed. "What do you mean, I can't fire you?"

"You can't fire me," he repeated, ignoring the sparks of anger in her eyes, "because I've got a no-cut contract."

"What does that mean?" Victoria frowned into his grinning face. She no longer cared about showing her ignorance of business matters.

"What that means," he said, tapping her gently on the nose, "is that you can't fire me. I can quit if I get a better offer from another team, but you can't fire me."

"What! Who on earth ever agreed to such a ridiculous one-sided contract?"

He chuckled. "Jake."

Victoria scowled. Her grandfather. She should have known! James had said her grandfather had wanted Gator, and she had known him well enough to know that he always got what he wanted. No matter what the cost. The only problem was, her grandfather was gone now, and she was the one stuck with the man!

A soft whimper escaped her lips. No wonder Gator looked so pleased with himself. He must have known all along that she couldn't get rid of him.

He had deliberately egged her on, taunted her and embarrassed her. And she had behaved like an absolute fool, playing right into his hands. Victoria glared up at him, resenting the fact that for the foreseeable future her destiny seemed to be tied together with his.

"Do you mean to tell me I'm stuck with you?" She realized she was hardly being polite, but at the moment she really didn't care. He burst out laughing and gave her shoulders a gentle squeeze.

"Hey, it's not that bad. You could've been stuck with Rodney."

"Roger," she corrected automatically. Gator had a point. Although at the moment she had the feeling she was caught somewhere between the devil and the deep blue sea.

"Oh, boy." He sighed dramatically. "I can tell you're really mad at me now."

Frustration slumped her shoulders. Now what was she supposed to do? Her thoughts whirled for a few moments. No matter what she did, she was stuck with this man. She needed him, and not the other way around. He could walk away any time he pleased, but she couldn't get rid of him no matter what! Like it or not, she was going to have to make peace with him.

What was she going to do? For a moment, she toyed with the idea of telling him the whole truth. If he'd let her improve his image so she could sell the team, he'd still be able to go on to another coaching job. Why should it matter to him who he coached for as long as he had a job? And certainly improving his image couldn't hurt. He might even come out ahead of the deal.

Victoria rolled the idea around in her mind, sorry now for the way their initial meeting had gone. With a resigned sigh, she decided to take a chance. What did she have to lose? Nothing, at this point. Nothing at all. She'd already lost everything. Everything except her pride. And right now, she couldn't hang on to a worthless emotion that wasn't about to support her or put food on the table. She'd have to take the gamble, tell him the truth and hope he understood the situation.

"No, I'm not mad at you." Shaking her head, Victoria tried to swallow back the tears of frustration that welled up in her eyes.

"Are you going to cry?"

Victoria shook her head furiously, not wanting to admit that was exactly what she was going to do. She was just so tired of the whole blasted mess.

"Oh, Tori," he whispered softly, dropping his arms to her waist to gather her close. She tried to hold herself stiffly, not wanting to admit how good it felt, how comforting it was to be held in his arms. His hands splayed around her waist and Victoria was momentarily paralyzed by the touch of his hand. The material of her suit seemed to melt away under his touch.

"Why don't you tell me the whole story from the beginning?"

She looked up at him, not certain why she was standing there, yearning to open herself up to him. Why did she feel a sudden need to tell him things she'd kept locked inside herself for so long? Things she hadn't told anyone. Maybe it was the sudden change in him that did it.

She hadn't been prepared for the range of emotions he'd shown. He had surprised her and caught her off guard. She'd expected Gator McCallister to be one thing, when in fact he was many things. At first, this afternoon, he'd been angry and resentful, then teasing and taunting. When he had found her with Roger he seemed jealous and protective. And now he was gentle and sympathetic. Where was the hard, tough-talking football coach? she wondered with just a touch of resentment. Him, she was certain she could handle. Maybe. But this warm, sensitive, utterly appealing man was a totally different story. A sigh lifted her shoulders. She feared she didn't have a prayer with this one.

"Tori?"

Victoria nodded, then relaxed her head against his chest, savoring the masculine scent of him. She was too tired to argue anymore.

"I have to sell the team. I . . . I just don't have the money to keep the Cannons going any longer." Her voice was muffled by his shirt and she felt his body tense. Embarrassment washed over her.

"Is that why you sold your furniture?" His voice was incredulous and he held her at arm's length, studying her carefully. "To keep the team going?"

She nodded.

"For God's sake, Tori," he yelled, startling her. "Why the hell didn't you come to me sooner? Why did you wait six months!"

"Come to you?" she yelled right back, feeling her body stiffen with anger. "Why on earth would I come to you? I never even met you before today!" How dare he criticize her! Her lips thinned in annoyance. "I think I've managed quite well," she added with a hint of pride.

"Managed! You call selling everything you own managing?" He shook his head in disgust. "Of all the—"

"Now you listen to me, Mr. McCallister!" She stepped out of his arms and glared up at him. "I've had just about enough of your insults and your taunts, not to mention your opinions. I've done the best I could with what I had to work with and I don't need you to criticize me." Anger shot through her veins and unshed tears filled her eyes. Victoria turned away from him. The last thing she needed at the moment was to go another round with him.

"Oh, Tori," he growled, grabbing her around the waist and hauling her close to him again. She tried to struggle free and brush her tears away at the same time.

"Come on, I'm sorry." His arms tightened around her body until she was nestled firmly against him. She was stunned at the way her body seemed to fit so perfectly to his. The fight drained out of her and her anger melted away as another more powerful emotion tore through her. His nearness sapped her strength and she relaxed against him, fearing her trembling limbs would collapse under her if she didn't.

"Don't cry. We'll work it out." His voice was seductively soft and her body responded. The connection between them was electrifying.

"We!" she echoed dully, not certain she had heard him right. She raised her head and looked at him carefully. "What do you mean, we?"

"I thought we could work out a deal." He smiled down into her confused face and Victoria inhaled sharply. Just what she needed, another deal from a man. Roger had wanted her house, but she had a vague idea what Gator wanted was a bit more personal.

Why on earth had she ever opened her mouth? Hadn't she learned from past experience? Everyone, or at least everyone she had considered a friend, had wanted something from her. That is, when she *had* something. It was funny how all her friends disappeared once she didn't have anything left anymore. Gator McCallister was apparently the same, only his tactics were just a bit different.

"Mr. McCallister," she said coldly. "Roger has already offered me that deal. I'm just not interested."

Gator drew back as if she had struck him. "You know, Miss Victoria Louise Fairchild, you are the most hot-tempered, stubborn, pigheaded woman I've ever encountered!" he roared. "What kind of man do—"

"Me!" she yelled, glaring up into his face. "Hot-tempered? I'm not the one who's—you're the one who's cantankerous and overbearing and—" His mouth stopped her words, coming down over hers so suddenly she had no time to protest. She lifted her arms to protest, to push him away but the moment his lips covered hers, she gasped, knowing in that instant she had fallen over the edge of reason where he was concerned.

His mouth ignited her senses and an inferno burst through her, halting all protests. Her breath caught in her lungs as his mouth tempted her, drawing her lips eagerly to his. Her hands moved around him and up the muscled contours of his back. She laced her fingers through the thick mat of his hair, savoring the silky softness.

His big hands circled her waist and hauled her once reluctant body against him. She knew she should protest, push him away, but she could no longer think about anything but the pleasure exploding through her.

She was aware only of the moment and the man in her arms. He tasted warm, wonderful and masculine. She felt herself grow soft and unresisting in his arms as need churned through her, leaving her breathless and weak-kneed.

Greedily, her hands ran the length of his back, his fingers savoring the muscular strength of him beneath the cool material of his shirt. She traced a path with her hands, knowing the sensation would be forever branded in her mind.

Perhaps she had known from the moment she had laid eyes on him that there was something different about him. The air had arced and sizzled between them with an electricity that didn't make sense until this very moment.

Clinging to him, her breath mingled with his as his tongue dipped and darted, enjoying the honeyed sweetness of her mouth. His massive chest moved against her breasts as he pulled her tighter, cradling her close. From shoulder to knee, everywhere he touched, he marked her with his body.

Her breathing stalled and an intense pounding throbbed through her. Instinctively she arched her body close to the warmth of him as his hands explored the soft lines of her back, the gentle curve of her hip.

With a soft moan, Gator pulled his mouth from hers, leaving her trembling with desire. His lips trailed across her cheek, leaving a flame of desire in their path. Victoria blinked, stunned and still reeling. She felt as if she had just slowly awakened from a trance.

"Oh, Lord," he whispered against her cheek. He lifted one hand to tease the skin of her neck and her breathing dragged again. "Dear, sweet, cantankerous Tori." He looked down at her.

She could see the desire sparkling in the depths of his ebony eyes. She knew she should have been frightened, but then she realized, she knew, her own eyes must reflect the same emotion. The thought brought a flush of embarrassment to her cheeks.

She swallowed and tried to calm her senses. Slowly and carefully, Gator was tackling all the walls of her defenses. She wasn't sure she could handle him. Or the emotions he stirred up inside of her.

"Now don't get mad at me again," he said, keeping his arms firmly around her. "That's the only way I could think of to shut you up so that I could finish what I had to say." He raised her chin with one hand, but she refused to meet his eyes, afraid he might see the desire that was still swirling uncontrollably through her.

"Now you listen to me, Victoria Louise Fairchild!" he ordered, in the same voice he had used that afternoon at the football field. But she was no longer frightened of him. "I don't make indecent propositions to women. If I want something, or someone," he added heavily, "I go after it fair and square. What I'm offering you right now is a business proposition, nothing more, nothing less. It's strictly business."

A business proposition. Could she believe him? Could she trust him? Should she? What kind of business proposition did he have in mind? Victoria looked up at him and all she could think about were his lips on hers. The warmth of his body as he held her close. For a moment, she longed to relive the moment over again. Then her senses righted. She ran a hand across her eyes and forced her mind on the right track. "All right." She nodded. "I'll listen to what you have to say."

"Good." He slowly trailed his hand up and down her back, which made her arch her body with pleasure. "I don't want you to sell the team, Tori."

She sighed and tried to ignore what his hand was doing. Must the man keep touching her? she wondered darkly. How on earth was she supposed to think about business when her mind was on him and the effect he was having on her?

"I don't want to sell the team, either." His hand tiptoed up and down the length of her spine and Victoria swallowed hard. "I . . . I don't have any choice."

His fingers slid upward to cup the back of her neck and his eyes settled on her mouth. Her breath slowed. For a moment she was certain he was going to kiss her again. And then she was disappointed when he didn't.

"What's your proposition?" she asked softly, knowing the proposition that was going through her mind at the moment was definitely *not* businesslike.

"You seem to think you can't sell the team until you improve my image." He shrugged. "Maybe you're right. I'll let you work on my image if you promise to wait a month before putting the team up for sale."

She shook her head, not quite understanding what he was getting at. "Gator, what possible difference could a month make? Nothing's going to change. I'll still be in the same position I'm in right now."

"Tori, when your grandfather brought me to the Cannons he did it because he thought I might be able to turn the team around. I've been making some progress, but it's slow. Give me a month. If we win a few games, you might be able to get a better offer for the team. It's a lot easier to sell a winning team than a losing one. Besides—" he grinned "—who knows what could happen in a month? If my image is improved, it's bound to help you sell the team. What do you say, is it a deal?"

What he said made sense. It certainly would be easier to sell a winning team than a losing one. If Gator allowed her to improve his professional image, particularly now with this no cut-contract, she might have an easier time convincing someone to buy the Cannons. It was certainly worth a try.

"Gator, why are you doing this?" She looked up at him and tried to read his expression. "You hold all the cards. If you really wanted to you could tell me to go to—"

"Victoria!" he scolded, reaching out to ruffle her hair. "Don't cuss."

She smiled. "All right, but tell me why." She couldn't understand why he was doing this. He had to have a reason, but what?

"Because ladies don't cuss," he said in his most polite voice and she grinned.

"That's not what I mean and you know it."

He gave an exasperated sigh. "Let's just say I'm repaying a debt. Jake did a lot for me. I owe him this one."

"Gator, I don't want your charity," she whispered, feeling an acute wave of shame. She didn't want anyone feeling sorry for her. Somehow she'd find a way to manage.

"Damn it, Tori," he growled. "It's not charity. If you give me a month, I'll let you improve my image. You're doing something for me, and I'm doing something for you. It's a fair deal all the way around." He cocked his head and looked at her skeptically. "Unless you want to sell your house to Ronald so he can give it to Betty."

She laughed and shook her head. He was totally impossible. Charming, but impossible. "It's Roger and Bonni," she corrected.

"Who cares!" he bellowed. "Is it a deal? Or not?" His eyes searched her face and she smiled. If he let her improve his image, at least the image he presented to the public, she'd have an easier time selling the team. He knew it and she knew it. It would take at least a month to get the paperwork rolling, contact her attorney and look for a financially suitable buyer. One more month. What could it hurt? Her mind raced. She'd need enough money to keep going. All she had left was an antique broach her grandfather had given her on her eighteenth birthday. She had held onto it for sentimental reasons. But there was no room in her life for sentiment now. The broach had to go. She'd call Mr. Androk in the morning. He might as well pick up the broach as well as the glasses and save a trip. The sale of the broach should bring in enough money to keep her going for a month.

"It's a deal," she agreed.

"Good! Let's go," he said, grabbing her arm and pulling her toward the door. "I'm glad you're done fussing."

"Ladies don't fuss," she announced with a laugh, coming to an abrupt halt. He was back to being overbearing again.

"Well, do they eat?" he barked.

"Well, of course," she answered with a frown.

"Then let's go!" He grabbed her elbow again and started moving toward the door.

"Wait a minute," she cried, not willing to let him overwhelm her again. "Where are we going?"

Gator looked suitably exasperated. "Tori, I just told you. We're going to get something to eat."

If he was inviting her to dinner, at least he could have been a little more specific on the point. "Gator, I can't go anywhere dressed like this."

He looked down at her and frowned. "What's wrong with the way you're dressed? You look just fine to me."

She cocked her head and laughed, relieved that even at her worst, he didn't think there was anything wrong with the way she looked. "I couldn't possibly be seen in public dressed like this." Her face was set determinedly and Gator sighed and threw up his hands.

"All right, all right! But where we're going, they don't care how you dress. If they did, they'd never let me in." He laughed and shook his head. "If you want to change, go ahead. I'll wait. But don't put on anything fancy and don't take too long." He pouted. "I get cranky when I'm hungry."

"You? Cranky?" She looked properly appalled, wondering if what she'd seen of him for most of the day was his pleasant, good-natured side. The thought brought a smile to her lips as she headed down the hall and up the stairs. Her thoughts were swirling as if she were caught in a revolving door.

In spite of everything that had happened, Gator had given her exactly what she wanted. He was going to let her improve his image so she could sell the team. He was going to help her, in his own way, of course. She paused at the top of the steps and frowned as a skitter of uncertainty rolled over her.

What she still didn't know was what Gator McCallister was going to get out of the deal.

## *Chapter Four*

Victoria stepped from the shower and quickly dried herself off. Crossing to her closet, she pulled out a white linen pantsuit, certain it wouldn't be too dressy.

She deliberately chose to leave her hair down, brushing the golden strands until they shone. Finally, she replaced her glasses with her contacts. Peering at her reflection she had to admit Gator was right. The lenses did do something for her eyes. She wasn't beautiful, but she did feel pretty. Gator made her feel pretty.

Victoria smiled at her reflection. There was something earthy and physical about the man that seemed to stir primitive desires within her. Funny, she'd never felt that way before. Victoria sighed. Gator was so different from the men she usually encountered.

Not that there had ever been a big romance in her life. While she had dated Roger on occasion, he was an acquaintance, not a romance. They had come from the same background, grown up together and had shared the same circle of friends. It was only natural that they gravitate toward each other. But in all the years that she had known Roger, she had never felt anything close to what she had felt for Gator in just a few hours.

It was odd because she and Gator were not anything alike. They had absolutely nothing in common, other than the football team. They came from two totally different worlds. Yet she felt totally comfortable with him. Well, she mentally corrected, she felt comfortable once she had gotten past the crusty exterior and saw the real man underneath.

Gator was unlike Roger in another more important way. Roger was only coming around because he wanted something from her. The only thing Gator seemed to want was to help her. Victoria shook her head. It was still hard to believe.

A smile curved her mouth. At a time in her life when she had begun to believe that everyone wanted something from her, along came a man who wanted nothing more than to help her. Even if his actions were only because he felt indebted to her grandfather, at this stage, she was not too proud to accept help. How could she refuse? Victoria chuckled softly. It was ironic that help would come in the form of a man that she knew barely a few hours, and who was her total opposite in every way.

"Victoria?" James knocked gently on her bedroom door. "Victoria? Are you almost ready? The coach is downstairs pacing the wood off the floors and mumbling under his breath. I can almost see the steam rising from beneath the study door."

She slipped her feet into a pair of strappy sandals then grabbed her purse. "I'm ready, James," she announced, opening the bedroom door. Although she had showered and changed quickly, it was obviously not quick enough.

"Oh, James." She stopped at the top of the steps and turned to him. "You'd better call Mr. Androk and tell him I want to sell the diamond and emerald broach."

James raised his brows. "The broach? That's the last piece of jewelry you have left." There was a sadness in his voice and Victoria smiled and reached out to pat his arm.

"Don't worry, James. It's going to be all right. The coach is going to help us."

James smiled and nodded his head, obviously pleased. "He's a good man, Victoria. Your grandfather thought very highly of him, even if they did go quite a few rounds together."

Victoria laughed and headed down the stairs. Knowing how stubborn and pigheaded her grandfather had been, she would be hard-pressed to pick a winner if Gator and her grandfather had come to blows. Gator was very much like her grandfather.

"It's about time!" Gator stood at the bottom of the stairs, his hands stuffed into his pockets. His gaze moved over her, touring the white pants and matching jacket. She noticed his eyes seemed to caress the heavy curtain of blond hair that fell in wispy curls to her shoulders. "Honey," he murmured, taking her hand, "you look beautiful. It was worth the wait."

"Thank you," she whispered, wondering why the simplest compliment from him set her heart racing.

"James, would you like to join us for dinner?" Gator asked, never taking his eyes from hers.

"No, thank you, coach. I've got a few things to take care of here. But I appreciate the offer." James practically beamed.

"James, do you think I could borrow a towel?" Gator looked a little sheepish and Victoria sent him a curious glance. What did he need a towel for?

"Certainly, coach." James turned crisply on his heel and headed for the main linen closet, obviously not in the least bit surprised by the strange request.

Victoria turned toward Gator. "Gator, what do you need a towel for?"

He smiled down at her. "You'll see in a minute. I thought I said nothing fancy." He lightly ran a finger down the lapel of her suit jacket. Although he hadn't actually touched her, she found her heart had begun to hammer like a machine gun.

"Gator, this isn't fancy, not really. It's just a suit."

"Don't you have any jeans?" he grumbled, inspecting the crisp lines of the suit again.

"No, I'm sorry. I don't." Why did she feel overdressed all of a sudden? Lord, she hoped wherever they were going, she wasn't going to embarrass him. Perhaps his idea of fancy and hers were not exactly the same thing.

"How about a sweatshirt?"

"Gator—" she laughed "—I don't have a sweatshirt either. Even if I did, I certainly wouldn't go out to dinner in it." Jeans and a sweatshirt to go out to dinner? she thought as he took the towel from James. Gator grabbed her elbow and escorted her out the door.

A vintage Corvette painted in a rainbow of colors sat in the long, winding drive. "Sorry." He flashed her an apologetic smile and held up the towel. Now she understood. He didn't want her suit ruined in his car. She ducked her head to hide a smile. It was such a gallant thing to do, she was touched.

"My other car is in the shop. This baby's an oldie but a goodie. I've had her nearly ten years now. I've been restoring her, but I'm not quite finished." He patted the roof affectionately before opening the passenger door. With a sweep of his hand, he knocked an empty pile of fast-food containers to the floor and draped the towel over the seat before helping Victoria climb in.

He coiled his long frame behind the wheel and started the motor. The car roared to life and Victoria jumped, raising her hands to her ears in a protective gesture.

"I haven't had a chance to fix the tail pipe yet," he yelled over the roar. "If the smell bothers you, open the window."

"What?" She tried hard not to cough.

"Open the window!"

Victoria nodded and pulled on the handle but it came off in her hand. Gator muttered under his breath, leaned over and yanked the window down with his hand.

"Stick your head out the window!"

"Excuse me?"

"I said, stick your head out the window," he yelled, his voice booming over the noise of the car.

Wide-eyed, Victoria stared at him for a moment. He couldn't be serious. Was he teasing her again? One look at his face told her he was serious. She turned and leaned her face out the window, taking a deep breath of the cool fall air.

She thought about her own immaculate little car. It ran efficiently, was wonderful on gas mileage and had never been defiled by fast-food wrappers. It was also about to be repossessed.

Victoria smiled and shifted her frame. The vinyl bucket seats were ripped and a corner was digging into the back of her leg. She tried to adjust herself more comfortably, then realized after a moment that comfort was something she would not find in this vehicle. Deafness perhaps, but not comfort. For some reason, it struck her as funny and she started to laugh.

Gator glanced at her and tried not to smile as he maneuvered the car into traffic. She hadn't said one word about the car, at least not out loud. But he could just imagine what was going on in her mind.

"Splendid vehicle," she announced, searching her mind for something polite to say. Men were very funny about their cars. Her grandfather had had a stableful, but had preferred to drive around in one that wasn't in much better shape than this one.

Gator smiled as he pulled into the parking lot. She was trying to be a good sport. "She's a real beauty, Tori. This car is worth almost twenty thousand dollars."

"What!" Victoria's eyes rounded as Gator threw open the door and helped her out. "You mean this car is worth that much money?" She turned to look at the car through new eyes.

Lacing his fingers through hers, Gator nodded. "You know, Tori, you can't judge everything by how it looks on the outside. Sometimes you have to look below the surface of things. Take this car, for instance. You'd never know it to look at her. She's loud and a bit messy, but she's one of the most reliable, dependable cars you'll ever find. Not to mention valuable,'' he added with a bit of pride.

His words surprised her and her gaze flew to his. Why did she get the feeling Gator wasn't just talking about his car? She didn't have a chance to find out. He hurried her across the street, not giving her a moment to do anything but struggle to keep up with him.

"This place we're going to for dinner is real special, too.'' He pulled open the door to a rather brightly lit restaurant. The place was called Eduardo's. Or Vincenzo's, depending on which sign you believed. Victoria blinked, unable to decide between the two.

Gator motioned her to a booth and slid in beside her. His warm muscular thigh pressed warmly against hers, causing adrenaline to flood through her veins. Unnerved by his closeness, Victoria tried to pull her leg away, but found there was no place to go.

"Take this place,'' he went on, looking at her intently. "It sure doesn't look like much on the outside. But inside, now, that's a different story. They have the best food in the city and it's one of the cleanest places you'll ever find. But a lot of folks won't ever know that because they won't take a chance. They won't look below the surface. They'll walk by, take a look at the outside and decide it's a dump.''

Dragging her eyes from his, she rolled his comments over in her mind. She was almost sure he was referring to something other than his car and the restaurant.

Victoria glanced around. Gator was certainly right about the restaurant. Although not modern in any sense of the word, the place was immaculate, from the shiny red-checkered tile to the gleaming Formica tabletops. Crisp, freshly laundered napkins were neatly folded at each place. The aroma of something heavenly filtered through the air.

"Where you been, boy?" a booming female voice called. The waitress, clad in a pink-checkered uniform, marched to the table and slapped two menus down. The woman was scowling at Gator and he grinned sheepishly.

"Sorry, Glory, I've been busy. Real busy." He nodded toward Victoria. "This here's Victoria. She's the new owner of the Cannons." He reached out and squeezed Victoria's hand, eliciting an embarrassed smile from her. "This is Glory, best waitress in the city."

"Hmph!" Glory commented, stepping back to examine Victoria more closely. Victoria sat politely, letting the woman's steely blue eyes go over her, feeling very much like a butterfly under a microscope.

Finally Glory smiled at her. "Listen, honey, you watch out for this one." She shook her finger at Gator. "He's a mean cuss, but you look like you can handle him. Just don't put up with any of his nonsense." Glory's smile widened and Victoria smiled back. "He's all bark and no bite. Don't you pay any attention to all those rumors about him. A sweeter man you'll never find."

Victoria couldn't believe it. Gator McCallister was actually blushing, right up to his ears!

"Come on, Glory," Gator muttered with a smile. "You're going to ruin my reputation."

Glory shook her head. "Not a chance. Someone else already took care of that for you." One blond brow lifted and she looked at Gator intently.

"Glory," he growled, casting a sideways glance at Victoria, who looked from one to the other in confusion. Why did she get the feeling she had just missed something important?

"Gator, this little lady looks like she'd blow away in a good wind! We better get some food in her, something to put some meat on those pretty bones." Glory reached out and patted Victoria's hand. "Don't worry, we'll fix you up. It's not good to be so skinny." Glory patted her ample bosom and let loose a chuckle. "Not that I've ever had that problem." Laughing heartily, she snatched the menus off the table and marched off.

"Don't we get to order?" Victoria asked.

Gator laughed. "Glory will bring us something wonderful. Don't worry. I guarantee you'll love it." His gaze locked on hers.

Did he have to look at her so intently? she wondered, trying to measure her breathing and still keep her eyes on his. She braced herself as her senses reacted. The forced confinement of the booth, not to mention Gator's warmth and closeness, were making her feel just a bit light-headed. It was a feeling she wasn't used to, and didn't quite know how to handle.

"Do you have a special man in your life?" Gator asked suddenly, as he adjusted his frame more comfortably in the booth.

His question took her by surprise and she blinked rapidly, nervously pushing back her hair. "No. No special man." Her answer seemed to please him, and his grin widened.

"Why?" She looked at him, suddenly curious. What did he care if she had a special man in her life? Just the thought that he might be interested in her caused a shiver to ripple up her spine.

"What about that Rodney character?"

"Rodney?"

"You know, lover boy, the one who wants your house."

Victoria laughed. "You mean Roger?" She shook her head. "There's nothing very special about Roger. I think he's out of my life for good."

"He is," Gator announced firmly, leaving no doubt that the matter was settled. Crossing his arms over his chest, he surveyed her intently. "I like your hair down." He frowned. "Where's your glasses?"

She smiled. She had wondered if he would notice, and she was decidedly pleased that he had. "Well, since someone once told me I looked like a startled owl with them, I decided to wear my contacts."

"I like it." He reached out and covered her hand with his. A trail of gooseflesh winged up her arm and she tried to ignore his gaze as it slid over her. His eyes seemed to warm every place they roamed. The heavy air grew still and she shifted uncomfortably.

"No special man?" He sounded pleased, she noted, with a quickening of her heart.

"What about you?" she asked a bit shyly.

"No." He tried not to grin, but failed miserably. "I don't have a special man in my life. Unless you count my quarterback. Now he's real special. A real team player. I've got high hopes for him. He's the one who hurt his shoulder this afternoon."

"Is he going to be all right?" In all the excitement she had completely forgotten about the injured man. The mental image of him lying on the field caused her stomach to churn once again.

Gator patted her hand. ‘‘Don’t worry, Tori, the doctor said he’ll be fine.’’ He shook his head. ‘‘We’re just going to have to activate his backup.’’

Victoria drew her brows together. Perhaps she had misunderstood him. ‘‘But I thought you said it was his shoulder?’’

It was Gator’s turn to frown. ‘‘I did. And it is.’’

‘‘Then why are you going to activate his back up? Did he hurt his back, too?’’

A deep rumble of laughter rolled up the length of him and he thumped his hand to the table. ‘‘You are absolutely precious, honey. Absolutely precious,’’ he choked.

‘‘Gator.’’ Victoria stiffened, realizing he was laughing at her. ‘‘I don’t see what’s so funny.’’

‘‘Tori, honey, you’re a babe in the woods. If you’re going to own this team, we’d better teach you a little bit more about the game.’’

‘‘But I’m not going to own the team, remember? I’m going to sell it.’’ Had he forgotten their deal already?

‘‘I know, honey, but it wouldn’t hurt to learn a little bit more about the game.’’

She nodded. He had a point. She’d never had an interest in football before, but now the game seemed a good deal more interesting. Perhaps it had something to do with the man sitting next to her.

Glory arrived at the table and slapped two plates down in front of them. Victoria inhaled deeply. Baked pork chops swimming in a sweet mushroom gravy filled her dish. A side order of mashed potatoes, covered with a generous portion of the gravy, completed the meal.

"Now eat," Glory commanded, pointing to Victoria. "When you're done with this, give a holler and we'll get you a refill."

Victoria's eyes widened. She'd be lucky to finish what was on her plate, let alone ask for seconds. "I don't know if I'll be able to finish all of this."

"Just eat," Glory commanded in a no-nonsense tone.

Gator grinned. "Don't bother arguing with her. You won't win." He let go of her hand, much to her dismay, and dug into his food. Victoria watched in fascination. She couldn't remember ever seeing anyone attack food in quite the same manner. Gator looked as if he was refueling for a long winter hibernation.

As soon as she lifted a biteful of food to her mouth, she knew why. The chops were heavenly, baked to a delicate perfection, and they melted in her mouth.

"You were absolutely right." She wiped her mouth on her napkin. "This food is wonderful." Victoria would never admit to him that, had she happened by this place, never in a million years would she have come in. Not for any reason except it wasn't like the usual restaurants she had frequented. But now that she was here, had tasted the wonderful food and experienced the warm, pleasant atmosphere, she could see the restaurant through new eyes. Gator had a point. Perhaps she did need to look at things a bit deeper, and not just on the surface.

Gator smiled as he cleaned his plate. "Ready for more?"

To her surprise, she nodded. "I'd love some."

"Glory," he yelled, bringing the waitress to their table in a hurry.

"Be right back," Glory announced, snatching the plates up. "Knew you could handle this cuss," she threw over her shoulder. Her comment caused Victoria to frown, remembering something else the woman had said.

"Gator, what did Glory mean about someone ruining your reputation? Did someone deliberately do something to hurt your reputation?"

She noticed him tense, but he tried to hide it with a shrug of his massive shoulders. "You know how those things go. Sometimes they get blown out of proportion." He flashed her a smile. "It's nothing for you to worry about."

She only half believed him. She had a feeling she just hit on a subject that he didn't want to discuss. Or rather, didn't want her to discuss. There was more to it than he let on, she just sensed it. After spending nearly the entire day with him, she had a hard time reconciling the hell-raising reputation with the man sitting next to her. Sure, he was big, pretended to be gruff and was definitely surly, but underneath all that was a certain gentleness, a certain unmistakable sweetness that came through. Anyone who spent any time with the man could see that. So why the image problem? she wondered.

"Did something specific happen, Gator?"

A muscle in his jaw twitched and she knew she was treading on forbidden ground. It only increased her curiosity.

"What's done is done," he said tersely, breaking off a chunk of crisp French bread.

"But Gator, if someone's deliberately done something to make you look bad, you should do something about it." She didn't understand this abrupt change in him. He was hiding something from her and she knew it. But what? And more importantly, why?

"It's a long story," he grumbled in a none-too-friendly tone. "And I really don't want to talk about it."

"Gator." She reached out to touch his arm. Touching him made her suddenly so physically aware of him she almost forgot what they were talking about. Victoria looked up and found him watching her carefully. She could tell by his face that he felt the electricity, too. She began to withdraw her hand, but he reached out and held her fingers tightly against his arm. She took a deep breath and tried to shrug off the feelings filtering through her.

"If...if I'm going to help improve your image, you have to be honest with me. It's only fair. I've been honest with you."

"Tori," he muttered softly, "you are the most stubborn—" He stopped abruptly and looked at her. "All right," he agreed. "I guess it's only fair. I promise to tell you all about it. Later! Right now, I just want to eat and enjoy your company." His brows rose expectantly, but she wasn't willing to be put off so easily.

"Gator—"

"Later," he growled, as Glory set down their plates. "We'll talk later." He dug into his food, leaving Victoria to wonder just what it was he was going to tell her.

She found herself stealing glances at him as she ate. She was full now, and not nearly as interested in her food as she was in him. Victoria knew she probably shouldn't be feeling this way toward him. This was supposed to be just a business deal. But, she realized with a bit of shock, what she was feeling all of a sudden for this mountain of a man with the contrary disposition had nothing whatsoever to do with business.

Gator pushed his plate away abruptly. "Didn't your mother ever teach you not to stare?" He glared at her.

"What?" Her face flamed and she felt a bit of perspiration break out above her lip. She had been caught staring at him like a lovesick child! How embarrassing! She simply couldn't help it.

"Never mind." He laughed. "Do you want some dessert? Or maybe some coffee?"

She shook her head. What she wanted, she realized, was to know what he apparently didn't want to tell her.

"Ready to go, then? I better take you home. I've got a team meeting early tomorrow."

Gator slid out of the booth, picked up the bill then went to pay the cashier. Glory approached the table and cleared their plates.

"Thank you." Victoria smiled. "Everything was wonderful."

Glory nodded. "Always is," she announced, piling the plates on top of one another. "You like him?" Glory nodded toward Gator and Victoria swallowed hard.

"Yes." She found herself smiling widely. "I...I like him."

"Hmph! He's a good one, just make sure you don't go stepping on his toes." With that, Glory turned and stomped away.

"Tori, are you ready?" Gator was standing near the cash register, tapping his food impatiently. Victoria scurried from the booth and followed him outside.

The evening air had turned cool. Although only early October, the temperature had dropped a good twenty degrees since they'd arrived. Victoria shivered slightly as she walked in step beside him.

"Are you cold?" Gator asked, and she wondered how he could not be freezing with his sleeves rolled up and no jacket on.

"Just a little." His hip bumped hers and she shivered again. But not from the cold.

"You know," he said, pulling her close until his warmth overwhelmed her, "I'm not very good at small talk. If you'd say something, maybe I'd know what you're thinking."

What she was thinking would hardly be considered ladylike by any stretch of the imagination. Victoria tried to harness her rampaging thoughts. His nearness seemed to vibrate her senses until she felt as if she was stretched as taut as a tightrope.

"I was just thinking about your image," she lied. "And how we should change it."

He growled under his breath. "I have a feeling I might be sorry I ever agreed to this." He threw open the car door and Victoria got the distinct impression he was not pleased.

"Gator, I—" She stopped and looked directly into his eyes. He was just a breath away. His mouth seemed to beckon to her. Dark eyes, which had flashed with anger and chagrin, were now soft and gentle as they caressed her face. Every ounce of her skin knew the touch of his eyes as they roamed over her. She felt loose and at odds with herself, and she wasn't at all certain she liked the feeling.

The evening wind whipped around them, licking up her face and tumbling her hair. His broad shoulders cut off the moon's light, but a beam glanced off his features, highlighting the angles and planes of his face.

Gator lifted his hand to brush the hair from her face. She inhaled deeply. Internal chaos left her quivering with awareness.

He bent down and she watched in fascination as his mouth drew closer. Instinctively, she licked her own lips in anticipation, wanting nothing more than to reacquaint herself with the softness of his mouth. Gator's lips brushed across hers, as if testing for acceptance. Victoria gasped, stunned by the rocket force that raced through her.

He brought his lips back down gently over hers, but with no less passion than before. Raising her arms, Victoria circled his neck and clawed her fingers through the silky strands of his hair. She leaned against his masculine strength, wanting only to stop the shivers of desire that left her weak with longing. All too soon, he pulled his mouth from hers.

"Get in, Tori," he said softly. "You're cold."

Cold would hardly be the word to describe what she was feeling, but Victoria did as she was told, remembering to keep her head out the car window as he drove. It was impossible to talk with the roar of the engine. The silence was warm and comfortable as they drove through the now quiet streets of Chicago.

A contented smile settled on her mouth and she sighed happily. She couldn't remember the last time she had felt this good, so at peace. She knew without a doubt that the man sitting next to her had a lot to do with what she was feeling. Idly, she wondered what would have happened if her grandfather had not hired Gator McCallister.

The motor sputtered in the night as Gator pulled the car into her driveway and cut the engine. For a long moment he sat there, silent.

"Come here." Gator turned to her with open arms. Without thinking or worrying about whether her actions were polite or ladylike, she climbed over the bucket seat and into Gator's waiting embrace.

His shoulders tensed and bulged in unison as he hauled her closer to him. Her breasts peaked in response, straining and aching as she leaned her weight against his massive chest. With a determined effort, she tried to force her breathing back to a more normal pattern, but it was nearly impossible. His scent infiltrated the air she breathed. Her chin brushed against the rough texture of his chin. Flames of desires wound themselves through her, binding her to him.

Victoria laid her head against his shoulder. The soft cotton of his shirt stroked her skin as sweetly as any embrace. A wave of desire burst through her senses, radiating through each and every pore of her body. She was fully aware of the hardness of his thighs as she leaned against him. Tremors of arousal caused her to quiver.

"You're cold," he whispered, shifting his frame so that his back was leaning against the door. He pulled her with him so that she was pressed tightly against him. His hands roamed slowly, exploring the soft lines of her back and waist. Spurred by his actions, she allowed her fingers to caress the muscled tendons of his neck and shoulders. Instinctively, she arched closer to him, shocked at her eager and willing response to his touch.

He slid his hands up and down her arms and she felt delicious sensations ripple across her delicate skin. Her mind refused to work as her emotions and senses took over. She couldn't put a coherent thought together. All she could do was feel. And what she was feeling left her giddy with desire, wild with longing. Shocked at her wanton reactions, Victoria turned her face into his chest, burrowing deeper against his shirt so that he wouldn't see her longing, wouldn't see the effect he was having on her.

"Tori, about this image thing..."

She lifted her head, realizing that he was about to tell her something important. It was impossible to read his expression in the darkness of the car, but she felt his body tense. She was so close she could feel every muscle move.

Raising a hand, Victoria guided his chin toward her. She wanted to make it easier for him. He had been so quick to offer his help and assistance. It was only fair. What else did she have to offer him in return, except her help.

"Tell me," she whispered, aching for him and wanting to know what had caused the sudden sadness in his dark eyes. She held his gaze, knowing that if she didn't he probably would never tell her. She wanted to know, had to know what had caused the sadness.

"Please?" She stroked his chin. His face was rough and flecked with the stubble of his dark beard, but she was certain she had never touched anything so wonderful.

"I don't like to talk ill about anyone—my wife—" He stopped abruptly.

She exhaled sharply. "Y-you're married?" The thought had never entered her mind. The mental image of Gator with another woman hit her with the force of a blow and she backed away. He caught her and brought her up close to him again, winding his arms tightly around her so that she couldn't move if she wanted to.

"Not anymore. I was married for a while, but things didn't work out for a variety of reasons. My pro career had just ended and it seemed as if I'd lost everything that mattered. I guess I went a little nuts. I've always had a bit of a temper but after I got hurt, well, my temper got a little shorter. I had a few run-ins with my players and the next thing I knew the press picked it up. They made a mountain out of a molehill, if you want to know the truth. They painted me out to be a step away from a padded cell. Hell, Tori, I wasn't crazy, just . . . just . . ."

"Hurt?" She felt an instant bond to him, suddenly understanding. Someone *had* stepped on his toes, and his heart. She understood perhaps just a little better why Gator appeared so hard and crusty on the outside. Gator, like her, had suffered, and his rough exterior was a barrier, a means of protection so that he didn't get hurt again.

He nodded. "I worked for her father as an assistant coach. After our divorce, she said some things and I said some things." He shook his head sadly and Victoria knew he was having a hard time. Gator was showing another, more vulnerable side and she felt a rush of warmth for him.

"The situation just got blown way out of proportion. Working for her father didn't help the situation. I couldn't go to another team because I had a clause in my contract that stated I couldn't change teams midterm unless it was for a promotion. My only hope was a head coaching position. No one in their right mind was going to offer me a head coaching position, not after all the bad press I received."

He turned to her and she saw sadness in his eyes. "That's where your grandfather came in. Jake heard about my troubles and offered me a job as head coach of the Cannons. Your grandfather really stuck his neck out, in spite of what everyone was saying about me. Jake took a chance on me, despite the fact that he was knee-deep in his own problems. I owe him, Tori. I really owe him." He sighed softly and turned to stare out the window again.

Victoria was silent, deep in thought. Now she understood exactly why Gator was going to help her. Gator really didn't want anything from her. He was just trying to repay a debt to her grandfather.

She breathed a sigh of relief as all her fears about him vanished. Maybe her grandfather had been wrong not to tell her the truth about their situation, but he *had* done something for her. He had hired Gator. Now that she had met Gator, she had a feeling her grandfather knew all along that Gator would help her.

"Gator?" She searched her mind for just the right words. "I have an idea."

He turned to look at her quizzically. "What kind of an idea?"

She tried to sit up, but he was unwilling to let her go. She relaxed against him. "Gator, if we improve your image, if we erase the image the public has of you, it might help turn your reputation around." He was silent for so long, Victoria began to fear she had hurt his feelings.

"Do you think so, Tori?" he said softly, and she expelled a pent-up breath.

Victoria lifted her head. His expression was so hopeful she felt her heart melt. As much as he pretended not to care what people thought, she could tell he did care, and cared deeply. "I don't see why not. It's worth a try." Her eyes locked on his. "Gator, I want to help you. It's the least I can do after all you've done for me."

"Honey, I haven't done anything for you," he protested, dropping his chin to her head and inhaling deeply. "You know, you sure smell good. For a prissy dame," he added softly, and she knew that the moment was past, at least for now. He was going to help her, and she was going to help him, and that's the way it was going to be. But right now, he didn't want to talk anymore about it, and she understood.

"Where do you want to start?" His words echoed loudly in the darkness and Victoria frowned up at him. She was still floating somewhere on cloud nine, trying to figure out why his nearness sensitized her so.

He chuckled softly. "My image. Where do you want to start?"

She thought for a moment. "First we can get you some new clothes and get your hair styled. That'll do on the outside. Then we can—"

"Hair styled?" He looked at her as if she had just told him she was going to sign him up for tap-dancing lessons. She tried not to laugh at his expression.

"Gator, if we give you a more professional appearance, people will take you more seriously." Even in the dark she could see his expression change as desire began to flicker in the depths of his eyes.

The short distance between them fairly crackled with electricity. Victoria held her breath as her heart pounded. She found her eyes riveted to his mouth, waiting, hoping. When it finally descended on hers, she sighed in satisfaction and relaxed her body against his. She eagerly parted her lips for him, wanting only to taste more of him. His tongue dipped and probed, fragmenting her thoughts into a million tiny pieces. His mouth continued its hungry search and she found herself yielding to the honeyed sweetness that caused her to shudder in ecstasy.

Desire burst forth like new spring flowers, and Victoria moaned in pleasure. Shyly, she moved her own tongue against his. He tasted exactly how she expected. Sweet and warm, and deliciously sensual.

Groaning softly against her mouth, Gator moved his fingers slowly and surely up her back, tangling them in the mass of golden hair.

Lifting her arm, she wrapped her hand tightly around his neck, pulling him closer.

"God, Tori," he moaned against her ear as he pulled his mouth free. "What will the neighbors think? We've fogged up the windows."

"I don't care what anyone thinks," she whispered huskily, pulling his mouth back down to hers. She was not yet willing to relinquish the pleasurable feelings that were rolling over her. She wanted more. And now! Gator gave a low moan and pulled his lips from hers. She ducked her head to hide her disappointment.

"Neither do I, honey." He stopped to grin at her, his smile warm. "But think of my image. Besides, I've got an early meeting tomorrow. Come on, I'll walk you inside before James comes out looking for you." He helped her from the car, lacing his fingers through hers. "I should be through tomorrow about two, should I pick you up?"

Sighing wistfully, she nodded her head and gave his hand a gentle squeeze. Tomorrow seemed like such a long time away.

They stood on the porch, holding hands. "You know, Tori," he said, shifting his weight nervously. "You're not at all what I thought you'd be. I guess I'm surprised."

Victoria laughed. "And you, Mr. McCallister, are not at all what I thought you'd be. I'm kind of surprised myself." She stood on her tiptoes and brushed her lips across his.

"Tori," he growled, dipping his mouth back to hers. "If you start that, I'm never going to get home." She sighed against his mouth. "Now, prissy lady, go on, scoot. Go on in the house and get some rest. We've got a big day tomorrow." He bent and gave her a quick kiss.

"You know, Mr. McCallister, one of the first things we're going to have to change is the way you order people around. It's really not courteous."

He stepped closer and pushed his face into hers. "Are you saying I'm not courteous?" he growled softly, brushing his mouth quickly against hers.

"You?" she echoed, swallowing hard and trying to ward off the mesmerizing pull of his lips. "Not courteous? Never!" she whispered softly against his mouth.

"Good. Now—go to bed!" he ordered, giving her back end a little pat. "I'll see you tomorrow."

Victoria nodded and watched him drive off. She smiled as he pulled into the street, leaving a trail of billowing white smoke in his path. As far as she was concerned, tomorrow couldn't come soon enough.

## *Chapter Five*

Although it was early afternoon, the look on Gator's face was as black as night and just as ominous.

"Tori." Gator met her eyes in the large mirror and gave his freshly washed hair a toss. "I know I agreed to this image thing, and I know I also agreed to let that Mr. Wesley fellow chop off my hair—"

"Style," Victoria corrected, trying not to smile as Gator shifted uncomfortably in the tiny styling chair. He had been twitching and moving and scowling ever since they'd arrived at the fashionable hair salon. After cutting off generous locks of Gator's dark hair, Mr. Wesley had announced in a huff that the only way to tame Gator's newly shorn curls was with an ample dose of conditioner, and had gone off in search of some.

"Style, chop, whatever," Gator growled, his face getting darker. "Now, I sat here while he flitted about waving his hands and oohing and ahing. But I'm not going to walk around smelling like a petunia garden!" He crossed his arms over his chest in protest and she smiled wider.

He was behaving like a petulant child. But, Victoria had to admit, he had been reasonably behaved, considering. He hadn't uttered any unrepeatables the whole time, at least not so that she could hear. And she had to admit, Mr. Wesley had oohed and ahed a lot, particularly when he'd found out it was the great Gator McCallister who was sitting in his styling chair. Mr. Wesley was apparently quite a fan of Gator's. He had recited play by play some of the highlights of Gator's greatest games. Gator hadn't seemed very impressed, even though the man had fairly swooned over him.

Gator had eyed Mr. Wesley's thin, fragile frame and flowing caftan, then muttered something under his breath that had caused Victoria to cringe. But Gator had allowed the stylist to fuss around him without so much as a peep. Until now.

"Ah, here we are, darlings." Mr. Wesley swept into the room, brandishing a bottle of unidentified green liquid. He poured an ample amount into his hands and rubbed them gleefully, casting a worshipful eye on Gator.

With a menacing look, Gator watched him. And Victoria watched Gator. She felt an explosion coming on.

"What is that stuff?" Gator cocked his head. He was surveying the bottle with a look that should have congealed the liquid on the spot.

"Conditioner, darling," Mr. Wesley cooed. "Golden-apple conditioner." Mr. Wesley sniffed the mixture and sighed appreciably. "Just the thing to tame you." He sighed, dipping his head for effect.

His words propelled Gator from the chair. "That does it!" he yelled, yanking the plastic cape from around his neck. With one quick jerk, he sent the cape sailing to the floor in a heap. Grabbing Victoria's hand, he started pulling her toward the door. "Let's get out of here!"

"But wait! Your hair!" Mr. Wesley wailed and stamped his foot. "It's not finished."

"The hell it's not!" Gator shot back, yanking open the glass door to the salon.

"What about your nails?" the stylist called, his voice clearly offended. "And your manicure? I haven't even started."

"Tough!" Gator yelled over his shoulder, giving Tori a shove to get her moving. "My nails are fine just the way they are!" Grabbing her arm, Gator pulled her along, not caring that her feet were barely touching the sidewalk.

"Now, Tori, I know you're probably mad at me," he said, not slowing his pace any. "I'm sorry about what just happened, but I just can't see myself walking around smelling like—"

A burst of laughter shook her and she stopped abruptly in the middle of the sidewalk. Curious pedestrians walked discreetly around her.

"What's so funny?" He peered down at her, totally perplexed. She looked at his face and started laughing again.

"You," she managed, wiping a tear from her eye.

"Me?"

"You," she choked. "I wish you could have seen the look on your face when Mr. Wesley came out with that bottle of conditioner.'' Victoria doubled over with laughter. ''Your face—you were so—'' She held her sides and stopped to catch her breath.

''I guess I did look pretty silly.'' He laughed softly. ''Tori, I just couldn't let him put that green goop on my hair. Golden-apple conditioner,'' he mimicked, his voice unnaturally high. A shudder shook his shoulders and she started laughing again.

''It could have been worse,'' she suggested, trying to keep a straight face.

''Worse!'' he bellowed, causing looks from curious strangers as they sidestepped around them. ''What could be worse?''

''It could have been purple-prune conditioner.'' She started laughing again.

''So you think it's funny, huh?'' he asked, grabbing her elbow and pulling her along the sidewalk. ''Well, Miss Victoria Louise Fairchild, it's your turn.''

''My turn!'' She came to an abrupt halt, but he paid her no heed as he slipped his arm around her waist and propelled her forward.

''Yes, your turn. Now I sat and let that—''

''Gator,'' she warned, giving him a stern look. ''Remember your image.''

''Image,'' he grumbled. ''I've got a feeling I'm going to regret ever agreeing to this. But you're not going to change the subject. I sat there and let him chop my hair off, now it's your turn.''

''For what?'' She let him lead her down the street, her curiosity getting the best of her.

Gator pulled her into a large department store, and dragged her up and down the aisles until he found what he wanted: a large round display of sweatshirts in a variety of colors.

"Gator," she gasped. "You can't be serious."

He smiled and crossed his arms. "Very serious." He picked out an army-green one and held it up to her. "This one looks about your size. Go try it on."

"But I've never even worn a sweatshirt," she protested as he pressed the garment into her hand and nudged her into a dressing room.

"It's about time you did. Now go!" He pushed her into the dressing room and pulled the curtain closed.

With a resigned sigh, Victoria pulled off her sweater and slid her arms through the offending garment. She almost groaned when she saw her reflection. The sweatshirt looked as if it would fit the entire Cannons team—it was enormous. The sleeves hung down past her wrists, and the waistband cradled her hips. He had to be kidding. She couldn't very well be seen in public in this thing.

"Gator," she whispered, peering through the curtain. "I don't think this is going to work."

"Let's have a look."

"You don't expect me to come out there in this?" Her tone was shocked, eliciting a chuckle from him.

"Either you come out or I'm coming in." Not doubting him for a minute, she sighed, pulled back the curtain, and walked out of the dressing room.

He inspected her carefully, pushing up the sleeves and tucking the waistband underneath. "It looks pretty good," he announced. "We'll take it."

"Gator!" She grabbed his arm. "I can't wear this! I look like—like a pregnant olive." She didn't want to add that no matter how inexpensive the garment was, she couldn't afford it.

He laughed and shook his head. "No, you don't, honey, you look just fine. Now hurry up and get your things, we've got a few more stops to make."

"A few more stops?" Victoria eyed him suspiciously, not liking the look on his face or the teasing tone of his voice. "It's your image we're supposed to be improving," she reminded him, wondering just what he was up to.

He grinned. "Stop complaining and hurry up." He gave her back a nudge and Victoria realized he was definitely up to something.

Gathering her sweater, she tried not to be embarrassed at her new wardrobe as he led her to the cashier and paid for her sweatshirt. She had to admit it was comfortable. The material was soft and warm against the brisk fall day, even if it did look ridiculous with her white slacks.

"Now what?" she asked, trying to keep the sarcasm out of her voice. "Paratrooper pants?"

"Tori, don't be rude," he scolded in his most polite voice. "Ladies are not rude," he reminded her, linking his arm through hers. "We're going to get you some jeans and a pair of boots."

She breathed a sigh of relief. Jeans she could handle. Boots, well, that was another matter. He stopped at another store. The window displayed an enormous assortment of jeans in different styles and colors. Gator frowned and muttered as he studied them, then finally dragged her inside.

"We're looking for a pair of jeans," he told the saleslady. "For a waist about this big." He held his hands in an impossibly small circle.

"That small?" the saleslady questioned, giving him the once-over.

"They're not for me, ma'am," he said politely. "They're for her." He motioned to Victoria with his thumb, and the plump, silver-haired woman looked at her carefully then heaved a mournful sigh.

"Such a pretty girl. What a shame."

Gator frowned. "What's a shame, ma'am?"

The saleslady winked at Victoria. "It's a shame she can't speak for herself. It must be a handicap having to haul you around everywhere to speak for her." She sniffed, then walked around Gator and took Victoria by the arm. "Let's go see what we can find, honey."

"None of those baggy ones," he suggested, ignoring the woman's exasperated look. "We want something nice and formfitting, to show off her figure."

The woman helped Victoria pick out several pairs of jeans in an assortment of styles while Gator roamed the store. Victoria tried on all of them, finally settling on two pairs that she really liked. She walked out of the dressing room to get Gator's opinion and found him behind the counter, lifting boxes for the woman.

"What are you doing?" she demanded, smiling. The man never failed to surprise her.

"Just helping out a bit. These boxes needed to be moved, so I moved them." He looked at her and let out a low whistle. "Turn around," he instructed, crossing his arms across his chest to enjoy the view.

Victoria turned around slowly, reveling in his appreciative stare. The jeans molded smoothly to her hips, falling tightly across her thighs and calves. There was a small slit at the ankle that showed just a bit of skin.

"Do you like them?" she asked, holding her breath.

He groaned softly. "Hell, honey, I love them." He turned to the saleslady. "We'll take them."

A strained look settled on Victoria's face and she tugged on his arm. "Gator," she whispered so as not to be overheard, "I can't afford all these things."

He turned to her, his eyes dark. "Victoria Louse Fairchild! When you're out with me, I pay. I don't care what we buy. I pay! I don't take money from women. Not for food, not for clothes, not for anything. You understand? I'm buying the clothes and you're going to wear them and I don't want to hear another word about it." He grinned down at her. "Besides, since I don't plan on drawing a salary for the next month, when you think about it, you are paying for these things."

It wasn't quite the truth, and she knew it, but Victoria nodded, not understanding why he was so touchy about her paying for things. She'd argue with him about it later when they didn't have an audience. She knew he must be living off his savings, and she didn't want to break him. Mentally, she totalled up their purchases so that she could repay him.

"Besides, it's not polite to look a gift horse in the mouth," Gator continued, peeling off a wad of bills and tossing them to the counter. "Don't forget about the hat," he told the woman.

Victoria stopped. "What hat?" Sweatshirts and jeans she could handle. But a hat? Well, a hat was an entirely different story.

"This hat," he returned happily, plopping a beige Stetson on her head. She could barely see over the rim. "That looks real nice, Tori. Now you look... beautiful," he said softly, his gaze locking on hers. "And," he added with a laugh, "not a bit prissy. Now you really look like Tori."

Pulling her eyes from his, she adjusted the hat more comfortably on her head. If he could sit in Mr. Wesley's chair and not complain, she could certainly wear a sweatshirt, a pair of jeans and a hat that looked as it it belonged in a B Western. It was the least she could do.

"What next?" she asked, as he took her packages.

"Boots, then lunch," he announced. "I'm starving." She visibly relaxed. Lunch she could handle. She'd reserve judgment on the boots until she actually saw them. He dragged her into a shoe store, ignoring her protests as he inspected pair after pair until he found just what he was looking for.

Yanking the boots down from the counter, Gator dropped them to the floor for her to try on. Shaking her head, Victoria kicked off her shoes and slid her feet into the soft leather. Wiggling her toes, she had to reluctantly admit they were comfortable, even if they did make her feel like an escapee from a cowboy movie.

"We'll take them," Gator announced with a happy grin. Without waiting for her to change back into her old shoes, he grabbed her arm and paid for her new boots.

"You like hot dogs, Tori?" he asked as he led her out of the store, oblivious to the hard time she was having adjusting to her new footgear.

"Hot dogs? I love them," she announced, watching her ankles wobble as she strode to keep up with him.

"Good."

Ten minutes later they found a corner booth at Ernie's and devoured the best hot dogs she had ever tasted. The place was tucked into a corner behind a large store. They had to maneuver through an alley to find the entrance.

"Is this another one of those places?" she asked, wiping a bit of mustard off her chin.

He nodded and took a sip of his root beer. "Yes," he replied, surprising her by instantly knowing what she was talking about. It was odd that they seemed to be on the same wavelength. She knew what he was thinking and how he was feeling without him even saying anything. "You know, Tori, it's hard to believe that you're the same woman who came storming into the tunnel yesterday full of spit and vinegar." He chuckled softly at her startled expression.

"Spit and vinegar!" she repeated, tossing her napkin at him.

"I knew right away you were Jake's granddaughter." He smiled warmly at her and reached out to cover her hand with his. "What I can't figure out is why you waited so long to come and see me." His fingers stroked hers and she shifted uncomfortably. All day there had been a warm camaraderie between them. The undercurrent of electricity was there, but not out in the open. Now, with his hand on hers, she felt her pulse begin to dance to a familiar tune. A tune that only played when Gator was near.

She sighed, wanting to make him understand. "Gator, when my grandfather died, I had no idea there wasn't any money left. I guess he tried to shield me from the harsh realities of life. I just assumed...well..." She shook her head. "When I found out I was broke, it was a shock, but nothing I couldn't handle. I never really cared about the money. I had grandpa and James and that was all I cared about. But my friends, or rather so-called friends, reacted immediately. Suddenly, I was an embarrassment. Poor Victoria, no money, no nothing. Without money, I wasn't worth their time. Or their friendship," she added softly as he tightened his grip on her hand.

"Those—" He stopped, catching himself before he said something he shouldn't have. He grinned sheepishly and she smiled, not wanting him to know it still hurt.

"I learned a valuable lesson. As long as I had something they considered valuable, I was worthy of their time. When I didn't, well . . ." Her voice trailed off. "I didn't think I had anywhere or anyone to turn to. It seemed as if everyone wanted something from me."

"Come over here." Gator patted the seat next to him and Victoria glanced nervously around the crowded restaurant.

"Gator, I don't think—Gator! What are you doing?" He got up, slid in beside her and put his arms around her. She tried to ignore the sudden lightheadedness his closeness brought on.

"Gator," she whispered, more unnerved by his closeness than the fact that they were making a public display.

"Honey, I guarantee you that these people aren't paying the least bit of attention to us. Now I want you to promise me something."

She looked into his eyes and realized she was lost. She'd promise him anything at this moment. Anything.

"What?" she whispered, wondering if he could see the longing in her eyes.

"I want you to promise me that you're not going to worry. You're going to improve my image and you're going to sell the team. Got it?"

She blinked and tried to smile, but inside she ached with doubt. "All of it, just like that?" She snapped her fingers in the air.

"Just like that." He reached out a finger and wiped a spot of mustard from her chin. "You don't need people who are just your friends because you've got something they want." He snorted. "Hell, those aren't friends, they're vultures, and a lady like you doesn't need people like that." He brushed his thumb across her lip and instinctively she kissed it.

He grinned suddenly. "You know what you need?"

"What do I need?" she asked, knowing full well that what she thought she needed at the moment and what he was about to offer were probably not the same things.

"Exercise!" Rising, he pulled her to her feet.

"Exercise!" She groaned. "Gator, I want you to know that whenever I get the unconscionable urge to exercise, I lay down until the feeling passes."

He chuckled softly and pulled her along. "A game of touch football is just the thing to get your mind off your troubles."

She groaned, loudly this time, causing him to laugh and hug her tight. She had a feeling she was about to learn all about football—the hard way.

"But she's a girl!" the little boy protested, casting a dubious eye at Victoria and giving the dirt a good kick with the toe of his shoe.

"I know." Gator sighed heavily. "But let's consider this our civic duty. Girls have to learn how to play football sometime," he announced to the entire circle of ten-year-olds that had been gathered at the park awaiting his arrival. The sun was winding down for the day, and the park was bathed in a honey-colored glow.

Victoria stood in the background trying not to grin as Gator charmed and coaxed them into letting her play. She would have been just as happy to sit on a bench and watch, but Gator was adamant. She was going to play!

"Come here, guys, let me tell you a secret." The boys huddled around Gator. Occasionally one would lift their head to look at her. Victoria smiled and tried to look pleasant, but she couldn't help wondering what Gator was telling them.

"It's all set, Tori," he announced, coming to get her.

"What's all set?" She looked at him skeptically. She wouldn't be surprised to learn Gator had volunteered her to be the football for the game. She could almost feel herself sailing through the air. She tried not to shudder.

"You can play."

"What did you do, bribe them?" She didn't miss the twinkle in his eyes.

"I did something even better." He grinned. "I told them you were my new boss and if we didn't let you play you'd fire me." He chuckled heartily as her mouth fell open.

"Gator!" She gave him a whack on the arm.

"Hey," he protested with a wide smile. "Don't complain. It worked." Victoria smiled in spite of herself. Apparently even ten-year-old boys weren't immune to his charm.

After a few hurried instructions, Victoria took up her position. If she understood Gator correctly, a boy, the one with the red hair and cowlick, was going to throw the ball to her. She was supposed to run with the ball and not let anyone catch her.

"The object is to hang on to the ball," Gator had stressed. "No matter what." So that's what she was going to do. Hang on to the ball. No matter what. And not let anyone catch her.

She poured all her concentration on the little boy with the red hair who had the ball and was going to throw it to her. But somehow she must have misunderstood, because the boy with the cowlick didn't throw the ball to her. He threw it to someone else. Not knowing what else to do, Victoria started running in the same direction as everyone else.

She heard footsteps behind her and tried to hurry but her foot caught on something and she stumbled. The breath was forced from her lungs as she was grabbed around the waist and tackled. Victoria tumbled to the ground, vividly aware that someone large was sprawled on top of her.

She closed her eyes and tried to catch her breath. This was exercise? she wondered dully. It was more like corporal punishment.

She opened her eyes to find Gator grinning down at her. Her arms were pinned alongside her head, and her jean-clad legs were trapped and tangled up with his.

"Gator," she gasped, fully aware of his hard, muscular body pressed tightly on top of hers. "I don't have the football," she stammered, acutely aware that she had probably made a complete fool of herself.

"I know, honey." He flashed her a lopsided grin.

Her concern at having his body pressed against hers in such an intimate way was all mixed up with her fear that she had embarrassed him. "I'm sorry," she whispered, knowing that her senses were on red alert because of his nearness.

"I'm not." His warm breath skated across her face and she looked at him carefully, not certain she understood.

"But—I thought you said—I thought only the person with the ball could get tackled."

"I lied," he returned happily, adjusting his frame more comfortably over hers. Her body responded instantly, tensing and tightening. She could feel every square inch of him and her nerves howled in silent desire.

His soft breath was ragged against her face as his eyes met hers. His lips were so close her heart nearly stopped. Even through the massive folds of the sweatshirt she could feel herself responding to him. Her body ached and swelled from the yearning in his eyes.

Silently, she gazed up at him, acutely aware that his own body was responding to the cry of hers. She stared at the broad expanse of his shoulders, which strained gently against the soft material of his sweatshirt. Her eyes went over his face. His features were so familiar now. His dark curly hair was mussed and tumbled from the wind and now fell boyishly across his forehead. His eyes, spiked by long lashes, were filled with longing. His lush mouth was so close, so inviting. She felt as if she was drowning in a sea with no escape. Victoria forced herself to hold his frank, steady gaze, knowing with each passing moment she was sinking deeper and deeper.

His eyes darkened suddenly and his breath caught. A warm current sizzled the length of her as she watched his mouth lower slowly toward hers. Her heart hammered and she braced herself as primal urges, raw and uncensored, throttled her. The weight of his thighs caressed hers, the material of their jeans a sensual barrier that only heightened her awareness. His fingers slid along the length of her neck, causing her pulse to ricochet in response.

Victoria held her breath, waiting for his lips to find hers, to offer a release from the sensations radiating through her. She parted her lips in eager anticipation as his mouth drew nearer.

"Hey, coach!" A voice called from overhead. "What are you doing down there? The other team intercepted and scored a touchdown!"

Gator groaned and Victoria's eyes widened. She saw the regret in his eyes and smiled. He rolled off her and her body immediately responded to the cool rush of air where just a moment ago he had blanketed her with his warmth.

Muttering something she couldn't hear under his breath, Gator pushed himself to his feet and extended his hand to her. Victoria rose slowly, pausing to brush the grass and twigs off the back of her new jeans.

"Sorry, Tommy." Gator shook his head. "Miss Victoria here was running the wrong way. I had to stop her." Gator flashed her a wicked smile as the boy grunted in obvious disgust.

"Girls," Tommy muttered, storming off to join the rest of the makeshift team.

"I think you need a few more lessons," Gator informed her, as he helped brush at her backside. There wasn't any grass left on her rear end, but that didn't seem to bother him. Victoria felt it would be exceedingly rude to point such a thing out to him, particularly when he was trying to be so helpful.

Victoria threw herself into the rest of the game, no longer caring that playing football in the park with a group of ten-year-old boys and one overbearing coach was hardly ladylike. She was having too much fun and enjoying herself too much to worry about being a lady.

When Tommy threw the ball in her direction, Victoria startled herself by catching it. Stunned for a moment, she recovered quickly and started running toward the designated goalpost. Anxious to make Gator proud of her, she ignored the calls and laughter and didn't stop running until she had reached her destination.

Laughing, Gator sprinted up to her. "I did it," she crowed, throwing herself in his arms. He laughed and shook his head.

"You sure did, honey." He picked her up and twirled her around. "There's just one problem, Tori." He set her down gently and looked into her eyes.

"I didn't drop the ball!" she protested before he could go on. "And I didn't get caught!" she declared, lifting her chin stubbornly.

"I know," he agreed, nodding his head. "But there's still a problem."

"What problem?" she yelled, throwing up her hands in exasperation.

He grabbed her by the shoulders and she noticed he was trying not to grin. "The problem is you ran the wrong way." He turned her around and pointed to the opposite end of the playing field. "Your goalpost is at that end."

Tori blinked in confusion and looked up at him. "Wh-what does that mean?" From the look on his face, she knew whatever it was it wasn't good.

"What it means is—well, you just scored six points for the other team."

"What!" Her face fell and she moaned, dropping her head to his chest. Laughing softly, he ruffled her hair.

Some days, she thought grudgingly, it was just easier to be a lady.

## *Chapter Six*

"Tori," Gator yelled up the steps, "we're going to be late! If you're not up, dressed and down these stairs in fifteen minutes, I'm coming up after you!"

Lord, the man was back! Victoria rolled over and attempted to force her eyes open. She had barely gotten her mind and muscles to sleep, and now he was back! No doubt to haul her around some more, she thought grudgingly. In the past two weeks she had done things and gone places she never would have imagined. After two weeks of Gator's intense physical activity—to take her mind off her troubles, he had assured her—she was ready to trade her aching body in for a new one.

Smiling dreamily, she realized Gator had taken her mind off her troubles. She couldn't remember when she'd felt so carefree or had so much fun. Grimacing, she mentally added, or ached so much!

"Tori!"

Victoria groaned and pulled the clock from the nightstand, straining her eyes to see. Was the man crazy? It was barely seven a.m.! The sun probably wasn't even awake!

"Go away!" she called. Shifting her weight, she groaned as her muscles issued a loud protest. Her body was in shock. Gator was the most physical person she had ever met. A sigh of pleasure lifted her lips. In more ways than one.

She had played touch football, jogged, gone bike riding, hiking, and yesterday—yesterday she had actually climbed on the back of a horse. A *horse* for goodness sake! Victoria grimaced at the memory and buried her head deeper under her pillow. Horses were for tax shelters, or racing, or polo, she thought glumly. Not for riding.

But Gator had different ideas. And had told her so as he'd helped her aboard Miss Lilly. Miss Lilly. Victoria's mouth pursed in remembrance.

They had driven out to the country, supposedly to look at a vintage car Gator had his eye on for his collection. After a quick inspection of the vehicle, which he proclaimed unacceptable, Gator had suddenly informed her that he'd made reservations for two horses. With a wicked grin, he'd announced that she shouldn't be afraid, he had picked out a very ladylike horse for her, in keeping with her image, of course.

Not that falling off a horse could ever be considered ladylike. But fall off Miss Lilly was exactly what she had done, and not just once. By late yesterday afternoon, Victoria had realized that the only thing ladylike about Miss Lilly was her gender. The horse had bucked, reared and made grotesque snorting noises through her mouth and nose, not to mention what Miss Lilly had done in the middle of a public park—Victoria wrinkled her nose. Well, she wasn't going to think about that now. Right now, all she could think about was the pain tightening her body.

Her back end hurt, her legs felt as if someone had peeled the skin off them and her ribs cried out from being jostled up and down. What on earth all this physical activity had to do with improving Gator's image, she'd never know and, she realized, she no longer cared.

The past two weeks had been the most wonderful and carefree days of her life. Gator was a warm, charming, complex man. She knew, without a doubt, that her feelings toward him had nothing whatsoever to do with business.

"Tori." Gator's voice barreled up the stairs. "James has your breakfast ready, and if you don't get your butt down here you're going to eat it cold! Do you hear me? We've got a big day ahead of us, now get moving."

Why didn't the blasted man go away? At least for a few hours, until she felt sufficiently recuperated to face the world.

"Gator." She pulled the covers off her head. "The stores don't even open for three hours. We've got plenty of time." They had planned another shopping expedition for this afternoon. With all Gator's practices and the time they had spent pursuing other things, they had never finished shopping for his wardrobe. Most of the things he had bought had been for her, much against her protests. She was no longer sure whose image they were improving, his or hers.

"I'm coming up!" The sound of heavy footsteps propelled her into action. She had no doubt he fully intended to march up and drag her bodily out of bed.

"All right, all right, I'm up," she yelled, brushing the tangled mess of hair out of her face. But not awake, she thought dismally as she slowly inched her legs over the side of the bed. Forcing each aching muscle toward the bathroom, she turned on the faucets. Stepping under the hot, steady stream of water, Victoria sighed and leaned against the wall, letting the heat of the water ease her aches. At least her scalp didn't hurt, that was something to be grateful for, she thought ruefully. A smile tugged at her lips as she smeared soap over her. The past few weeks she'd become almost a different person. More relaxed, more at peace with herself. Gator had brought about such a change in her, and not just physically and emotionally.

Physically, at times, it was hard for her to believe she was the same person. The stiff, restrained hairdo was gone, along with her glasses and conservative clothes. She almost always wore her hair down, or else tied it in back in a swinging ponytail. Her glasses had found a permanent perch on her nightstand, in favor of her contacts. She lived in jeans and sweatshirts, having accumulated quite a collection from Gator. Her smile widened. Some women received flowers and candy, Gator brought her sweatshirts.

She was much more aware of things now. She saw things differently, looked at things differently. Now she looked below the surface of things, as Gator would say. The man made her so physically aware of everything, particularly him. Just the thought of him heightened her senses. He was a wonderful, charming, man. A man she would never have known, had she not looked below the surface.

Emotionally, she found she had relaxed, too. She was no longer so concerned with polite and proper, but more with caring and kindness. Gator was the kindest, most caring man she had ever met. When he was around, all her problems seemed to vanish, or at least he made her feel as if they did.

After rinsing off, Victoria grabbed a towel and dried herself off. With great effort, she pulled on her clothes, grateful she didn't have to fuss with tiny buttons or elaborate hairdos.

It took an unusually long time to dress, and she finally gave up on her hair, brushing it quickly, then letting it fall free to her shoulders.

"Have you got a problem?" Gator asked with a grin from the bottom of the stairs as he watched her painful descent. He was dressed casually, in a pair of dark jeans that hugged his slim hips and long legs, with a shirt in stark white that offset the darkness of his hair. She never ceased to be amazed at the impact he had on her. Just the sight of him was enough to set her heart hammering.

"The only problem is my body," she moaned, as he reached out his arms to her. His shirt rode up and Victoria caught a glimpse of hard tanned flesh across the flatness of his stomach. The sight of his bare skin caused a tingle to curl her toes. Scarcely breathing, she allowed him to take her arm.

"I know what you mean," he said. "Your body's been giving me nothing but problems since I met you." His wicked grin brought a warm glow to her face, and if she could have found the strength, she would have whacked him. He leaned forward, kissing her soundly on the mouth.

"Now, come on," he coaxed. He slid his arm around her, slipping his fingers beneath the waistband of her shirt to knead the bare skin beneath. Warmth stole through her as Gator led her into the kitchen and helped ease her into a chair, totally ignoring her groans.

"What you need is the famous McCallister massage. It'll ease all those little aches and pains. It'll make you feel like a new man." He flashed her a look. "Or in your case, a new woman."

The idea of Gator massaging her body brought another flush of warmth to her face and Victoria ducked her head.

"I don't see what the big rush is, Gator," she grumbled, taking a sip of the hot coffee that James placed in front of her. "The stores aren't even open yet."

"Tori, if I'm not complaining because you're going to be dragging me from store to store again today, I think you could stop complaining about going horseback riding." He dropped into the chair next to her, and his leg brushed hers. Her body began to hum and Victoria smiled. She'd gotten rather used to Gator touching her somewhere. He was constantly patting her or hugging her. It was nice, she had to admit, even if it still caused her inner system to fly out of whack.

"Where are you two off to today?" James asked, setting down a bowl of oatmeal in front of her. Victoria made a face. She was not particularly fond of oatmeal. But it was cheap and plentiful, not to mention filling.

"Now quit making faces and eat," Gator admonished, picking up the spoon and handing it to her. "You need your strength."

She looked at him skeptically. "Why? What daredevil deed do you have planned for me today? Skydiving?"

James was chuckling softly in the background as he puttered around the kitchen. It amazed her the way James and Gator got along. You'd think they were bosom buddies. Always talking and laughing about something. She knew that if she expected any help from James where Gator was concerned, she was in for a disappointment. The lines had clearly been drawn, and James was in Gator's corner. Not that she minded. It was easy to see that Gator returned James's respect.

Gator laughed softly. "You know I'm afraid of heights, Tori. No, no skydiving today. I thought we'd drop by the hospital for a little bit before we go shopping."

"Hospital?" Victoria stopped eating. "Are you sick?"

"It's not polite to talk with your mouth full," Gator scolded, shaking his finger at her. "And no, I'm not sick. But Tommy, you know, the little kid from the park? He's having his tonsils out this morning and I promised his mom we'd stop by to see him. To sort of cheer him up."

Victoria nodded. She was no longer surprised by anything Gator McCallister did. He was warm and gentle, and had a heart as big as the state. There was absolutely nothing wrong with him or his image. Even though he liked people to think he was menacing and threatening, he was neither, and she knew it. Now all she had to do was convince the rest of the world.

"Finish up, now," he ordered. "I want to get there before they wheel him up to surgery. Make sure you bring a change of clothes."

Victoria's brows rose. "What do I need a change of clothes for?" She wouldn't be surprised to learn he planned on swimming along the muddy banks of Lake Michigan.

"Now don't look like that, Tori. I'm just having a few of the boys over tonight and I thought you'd like to come."

"Me? You want me to come to a party?" She knew she was grinning from ear to ear. Everything they had done together had started out on the pretense of having something to do with improving his image, something to do with the business at hand. Every day she would accompany him to practice, fully intending to go shopping afterward. At least she had intentions of going shopping. But before she knew it, Gator had somehow steered her into other things. This was the first time he had issued an open invitation without any pretense. It made her deliciously happy.

"Why are you so shocked?" he asked scrubbing his hand across his chin. "I figured after the last two wins it's only right I have some of the team over. The team's finally getting some favorable publicity. I thought you'd like a chance to get to know them a little better, particularly since you're the new owner."

Her face fell. That's why he wanted her to come. It was to meet the team. It was just business. Although Victoria had met quite a few of the players at the practices, the men were usually outfitted in their uniforms with their helmets masking their features. Besides, most of her time had been spent on the sidelines with Gator. Who could pay attention to any other man with Gator around?

"All right." She set her jaw rigidly. She could be just as businesslike as he was. "But only if you let me bring something, and I'd prefer to come home and change."

"All right. But, Tori, this isn't anything fancy. We usually just have sandwiches."

"Good. Then I'll bring the sandwiches."

"Fine. But I'll pay for them."

She opened her mouth to protest, but closed it quickly when she saw the look on his face. Gator was very sensitive about her paying for anything—not that she could afford it, but she thought it only polite to offer.

"Okay," she agreed, knowing better than to argue with him.

He smiled, picked up her bowl and cup and deposited them in the sink. "Make sure you bring James along. I invited him myself this morning."

Victoria nodded and sighed. Business or not, as long as she was with him, she didn't really care anymore what they did. She could no longer ignore the fact that her feelings for Gator had nothing whatsoever to do with business. If only he would give her some indication he felt the same way!

"Now, Tori, come on. Move it!" He sighed impatiently and pulled her chair out, to help her up. "I don't want to be late."

"Coach, you made it." Tommy's mother sighed with relief and Gator patted her shoulder.

"Now don't you worry, Mrs. Colin, Tommy will be fine. This is Tori, she's a friend of mine." The woman smiled at Victoria, who politely shook her hand.

"I'll be right out," Gator told her as he headed toward Tommy's room.

"Why don't we sit down?" Victoria suggested. It was clear to see the woman was very upset. They found two seats in a small waiting area near Tommy's room. Victoria noticed Mrs. Colin was twisting a handkerchief nervously.

"Have you known Gator very long?" Victoria inquired, searching for a subject that would get the woman's mind off her son.

Mrs. Colin smiled. "About a year. He came across the boys playing football in the park one afternoon and offered to give them some pointers. From that day on, he was at every one of their games. Even though it's not really an organized league or anything, the coach made the boys feel like what they were doing was really important. He's helped Tommy quite a lot." The woman looked away. "Ever since Tommy's father passed away, he's been kind of lost. They were very close."

Victoria nodded her understanding. She knew the feeling. She had felt the same way when her grandfather had died. But for a ten-year-old child, it must be even harder.

"The coach has been great with Tommy. And all the other boys," Tommy's mother added softly. "He takes time with them, talks to them. He's made them believe that they can do anything they want in life as long as they try hard and believe in themselves. He's been . . ." She stopped to dab her eyes.

"Wonderful?" Victoria nodded, knowing exactly what the other woman was talking about.

"Yes, wonderful. Tommy was scared to death about this surgery. But the coach told him not to be afraid. He's done so much for him—and for me," she added, meeting Victoria's eyes. "Last year I lost my job and we were almost evicted from our apartment. Within a week the coach had found me a job with the team's front office. He even paid the back rent on our apartment." The woman laughed softly. "He was mad as a hornet because I hadn't come to him sooner." She shook her head. "I never even thought to burden him with our troubles. He—well—he'd just been a friend to Tommy, but now he's become my friend as well." She smiled and patted Victoria's hand. "I'm so glad he found someone. You're so pretty. He's a good man. He deserves only the best."

Victoria opened her mouth to protest, to tell Mrs. Colin that her relationship with Gator was strictly business, but she didn't have the heart. It would be a lie. While she was certain that Gator probably thought their relationship was still only business, she no longer felt that way about him. Her feelings went far beyond that. But there seemed no point in bringing attention to the matter. At least right now.

"Mrs. Colin, he's doing fine." Gator's voice caused them both to look up. "He's going to be all right." Gator smiled reassuringly.

"Coach, I don't know how to thank you." Mrs. Colin took his hand and looked up at him.

"No thanks are necessary, ma'am. You just take care of Tommy. He's a good boy. If you need anything, you call me. The office will know where to find me." He patted her shoulder and nodded. "I mean anything," he growled, taking her hand.

Smiling, Mrs. Colin stood up and pecked Gator on the cheek. "Thank you," she whispered.

"No thanks are necessary. You run along, now. I told Tommy I'd send you in." He took Victoria's arm. "Now remember, if you need anything, you call."

"Gator," Victoria said softly as he led her down the hall and out of the hospital. "Did anyone ever tell you you're wonderful?"

He opened the car door and stopped to look at her. Absently, he ran a hand across his cheek. "Well, honey, to tell you the truth, people have told me I'm a lot of things, and they've called me a lot of things, too. But most of the time I just don't pay any attention." He chuckled softly. "Now get in, we've got a lot to do today."

Victoria was silent as she climbed into his car. She could tell he was clearly embarrassed about her compliment.

He looked over at her, his eyes shining in appraisal. "I've got to admit, Tori, you do something to those sweatshirts."

She nearly beamed. His compliments always had this effect on her. She wanted nothing more than to please him. It mattered a great deal what he thought of her, and what he felt about her, she realized suddenly.

"What you did for Tommy and his mother was wonderful. She told me about her job and the rent and—"

"Where to first?" he asked, effectively cutting her off her praise. Victoria understood. One thing she had learned about Gator, he wasn't comfortable with compliments. Not from anyone, unless it had to do with football or a game plan; then he positively glowed. He'd been glowing a lot these past few weeks, particularly since the Cannons had been winning.

"Well, we have a ten o'clock appointment at Gerold's on Michigan Avenue." That information brought a groan.

"More clothes, Tori?" He swung the car around a corner.

"Now Gator, we've set off to go shopping I don't know how many times and we just don't seem to get there. We have to go. Today. With all the publicity the team's been getting, a great deal of attention has been focused on you. It's important that you present the proper image."

"You know, Tori, I do own some clothes. I think I've even got one or two suits tucked away in the back of my closet."

"Well, of course you own some clothes," she acknowledged primly. "You certainly haven't been walking around naked." She knew she was walking a fine line. She certainly didn't want to hurt his feelings, or imply that his clothing wasn't acceptable. There wasn't one single thing about the man that wasn't acceptable.

"Naked!" Eyes wide, he turned to stare at her in disbelief. "I do believe we've loosened you up a bit. A few weeks ago I'd have bet my last dollar you'd never even thought that word, much less said it aloud." He was teasing her again, and she knew it. "Naked," he repeated again, slapping his hand against the steering wheel.

"All right." Victoria smiled and gave his ribs a poke. "Let's not get carried away."

Victoria stared at Gator's profile for a long time. Sometimes you have to look below the surface of things, he had told her more than once. Now she really understood what he meant. On the surface, Gator McCallister appeared to be one thing, but deep down, he was really something else entirely. It warmed her heart. She couldn't quite remember ever meeting anyone quite so special before.

"Where'd you say we're going now?" Gator asked as he stopped for a light.

"Gerold's, on Michigan Avenue." An unexpected wave of tenderness washed over her as she lifted a hand to stroke his cheek. The stubble of his beard was rough against her hand, and she savored the texture of him.

"What's that for?" he inquired, turning to her with a smile. "Are you trying to soften me up so I don't complain about trying on all those fancy clothes?" His eyes were lit with a teasing glint and she smiled.

"No," she said softly. "It's for being one hell of a nice guy."

"Victoria!" He admonished, widening his eyes. "Ladies do not cuss!" A ripple of soft laughter filled the car as he pulled into the parking lot and gave her a quick kiss. "But thank you anyway."

Gerold's, the most fashionable men's store downtown, had assured Victoria over the telephone that they would have something ready-made to fit a man Gator's size. She picked out two suits, one a gray pinstriped, the other a basic blue. Gator took one look at the stripes and grimaced.

"Tori, if I put this on, I'm going to look like I belong in prison."

She laughed softly and shooed him into the dressing room. "Go try it on." Muttering under his breath, he lumbered into the expansive changing rooms.

"Tori," he grumbled, stepping out, "the pants are too long and they itch." He was examining himself in the three-way mirror and she couldn't help but smile. What the man did for a pair of jeans was wonderful, but what he did for a suit was almost indecent. He looked wonderful. The jacket was cut expertly, fitting over his muscular arms and shoulders perfectly. Unconsciously, she reached out and ran her hands across his back.

"It looks wonderful." Her voice was a husky whisper as his eyes met hers in the mirror.

"If you're going to touch me like that, I'll wear this suit all the time. Itchy or not."

She flushed and pulled her hand back. They were in the middle of a public department store and she was behaving like a lovesick adolescent, something that was quickly becoming a habit whenever she was with him. She had to change the tone, and quickly.

"Gator, we'll have the pants hemmed and lined. The length will be fine and they won't itch. I promise."

While he tried on the other suit, Victoria moved through the store, picking out several pairs of slacks and sweaters. They gathered their purchases and she waited while Gator paid for his new things. She was shocked at the cost, but surprised that Gator made no comment. A sudden thought began to grow in her mind, making her just a bit uneasy.

Knowing Gator, she would have to broach the subject carefully. She had no wish to embarrass him, but she had to know. Victoria waited until they had locked all the packages in the trunk and pulled back into the lunchtime traffic before bringing it up.

The subject of money was a sensitive one, she didn't know quite how to broach the subject. The past few weeks they had spent a great deal of money. Gator's money. On an assortment of things. Her jeans and sweatshirts, not to mention her hat, dinners out, Mr. Wesley's. And now, today, all the money on the suits. It added up to quite a lot of money. Gator had never once complained, not even over the cost of the wildly extravagant gray suit.

She knew he made a good living, she'd signed his paychecks. But ever since he'd learned she was selling the team, he'd refused to draw a salary, no matter how much she begged or pleaded. With no regular income, she had no idea what he was living on. And here she had been spending his money like a drunken sailor!

"Gator, I was wondering . . ." Her voice trailed off and she flushed.

"What?" He took his eyes off the road to look at her. "What's wrong? From the look on your face, I've got a feeling I'm in hot water again."

"No." She deliberately pulled her eyes from his. "It's not that." She stopped, not certain how to proceed. The last thing in the world she wanted to do was embarrass him. Money was such a funny subject. When you had it, it seemed like you never worried about it. Not having it was what brought on the worries. She had never even considered the enormous amount of money he'd been spending. "I—" She stopped once again, afraid to go on.

"That does it!" He jerked the car to the curb and slammed on the brakes. "All right, out with it! Are you mad because I made a damn fuss about that gray suit? I'll gladly wear it every day, itchy or not, if it'll make you happy." He reached out and lifted her chin, forcing her to look at him. She dropped her eyes to her lap, suddenly embarrassed.

"I—I was just worried."

"About what?" His hand dropped to her shoulder and Victoria fought back the hypnotic spell his touch wove around her. She needed to get this out in the open.

"We've been spending an awful lot of money." She lifted her eyes to his. He blinked in confusion. She could tell he didn't have the faintest idea what she was getting at.

"So, we've been spending an awful lot of money. Go on." He was looking at her quizzically now.

"Well, you haven't been drawing a salary—"

"So? I haven't been drawing a salary and we've been spending a lot of money. So what? What are you getting at, Tori?" His eyes were riveted to hers and she licked her lips nervously.

"I—I was just wondering if you can afford all of this?" She made a vague gesture with her hand. He looked at her blankly for a moment, then threw his head back and laughed.

It was her turn to look blank. She really didn't see anything funny about this. But then maybe she just had a sour view about money.

"You're worried about how much money I have, right?"

She nodded, feeling her face flame under his amusement. He reached out and wrapped an arm around her neck, pulling her close.

"You're sweet, did you know that?" he asked, planting a soft bouquet of kisses on her face. "Real sweet, but don't worry, honey." He laughed. "I'll let you know when I'm down to my last million or so."

Victoria smiled at his obvious exaggeration, and brushed her cheek against his. She had a feeling he was just trying to ease her mind. Gator wouldn't tell her if he was hurting for money, his pride wouldn't let him. She made a mental note to curtail their spending, just in case.

"Now, if we're through trudging through stores, trying on clothes and spending money, think we can go back to the hospital? I'd like to check on Tommy."

Victoria shook her head. "Would you mind if I went home to get ready for the party?"

"Come on, I'll drop you off at home. James has got my address. Everyone's coming at seven. So why don't you come about six-thirty?"

Happiness filled her heart and she nodded. They would have a half an hour together. Alone. It was going to be a wonderful evening, she decided, snuggling closer to him. "I'll be there."

# Chapter Seven

James, are you sure this is the right address?" Victoria squinted and peered through the windshield as James pulled the car to the curb. They were in a very nice neighborhood, one of the priciest in the city. Victoria knew for a fact that apartments in these Gold Coast high rises were enormously expensive. She frowned and surveyed the neighborhood. This was not quite what she had expected.

"It's the right place, all right. Here, check for yourself." James handed her a slip of paper. She recognized Gator's handwriting and the address. This was the right place.

"I'm going to park the car, you go on up. I'll bring the sandwiches up with me."

Wide-eyed, Victoria stepped out of the car. This neighborhood was not quite where she'd expected Gator to live.

A uniformed bellhop quickly opened the door for her and she gave him a smile as he escorted her through the luxurious lobby.

Her thoughts were spinning fast as she stepped into the elevator. After a few moments, she found Gator's apartment. She glanced quickly up and down the halls. The carpeting was a plush mauve, the walls decorated with mirrors and expensive wallpaper she recognized as limited edition. It must cost a fortune to live in a place like this, Victoria thought. She took a deep, calming breath. She was suddenly and unexplicably nervous. She'd never been to Gator's home before, and didn't know quite what to expect.

This was ridiculous, she told herself firmly. Lifting a hand, she smoothed down her white gauze peasant dress. She had taken great pains with her appearance this evening. She had washed her hair, brushing it until it glistened, coaxing and curling the long strands until they fell with primitive abandon around her face. Her makeup had taken a bit longer than usual, and she'd taken particular pains to play up her blue eyes. The dress had been chosen with deliberate care. It was a hand-painted cotton peasant dress her grandfather had brought back for her on his last trip to Mexico. It was nearly transparent; the collar bared her neck and shoulders, then fell softly across her breasts. The waist was gathered and the full skirt fell just to her knees with a deep ruffle. She loved it and hoped Gator would like it. Other than the suit she had worn the first day at the field and the outfit she had begun the next day in, the only thing Gator had seen her in was jeans and a sweatshirt. For some reason, she wanted to look particularly nice tonight. She wanted Gator to be proud of her.

Inhaling deeply, she raised a hand to press the bell.

"Right on time." Gator pulled open the door before she had a chance to press the buzzer.

"Gator," she gushed, her eyes wide. "This place is beautiful."

He chuckled softly and pulled her inside. "From the look on your face I'd say you were expecting a tent with a dirt floor?" Her eyes flew to his and she blushed.

"Come on now," he said, pulling her along into the living room. "A few of the boys are here already. I want you to meet them." She tried to hide her disappointment. She had hoped to have some time alone with him.

"This here's Spitface," Gator announced. Victoria smiled and shook the man's hand, mentally making a note to try and remember which name went with which face. Now that she could see the faces without all the wire.

"It's very nice to meet you, Spitface," she said politely, trying not to cringe as the man pumped her hand like a spigot on an old well.

"Lighten up," Gator growled, pulling her hand free. She had thought Gator was large, but this man seemed to dwarf him as he stood looking down at the two of them. His size apparently didn't bother Gator.

"Sure are pretty," Spitface announced, casting an appreciative eye on her bare shoulders. "Isn't she pretty, coach?" Spitface turned to Gator, who scowled up at him. Obviously Gator wasn't pleased that Spitface found her pretty.

"Why, thank you," Victoria returned politely, flashing the man a wide smile. She bit back a grin when she noticed Gator's scowl deepen.

"You don't have to encourage him," Gator muttered in her ear. He gave Spitface a not-too-polite nudge, indicating his introduction was over.

"Gator," she teased, linking her arm through his. "Why do they call him Spitface?"

"Because he's a nose tackle and when he gets riled up during a game he spits at the other team's players." She noticed his words were coming out in a rush and he was acting peculiar. Gator mumbled something under his breath and she noticed he was scowling again, but this time at her.

"What?" she asked. "What's wrong?" His eyes were going over her slowly and carefully. Self-consciously she looked down at herself, fearing something was exposed that shouldn't be.

He grabbed her hand and pulled her back into the hallway. "Why did you have to wear a dress?" His frown deepened. "What happened to your jeans?"

"Gator, what's wrong with this dress? Don't you like it?" She had thought, under the circumstances, a dress would be more suitable for a party. But apparently she had made a mistake, because judging from the look on his face, he didn't like her dress.

His eyes narrowed as they took in her bare shoulders, the way the dress draped softly, outlining the curve of her breasts. He muttered under his breath again and suddenly reached up and pulled her dress up atop her shoulders so that it crimped and bunched across her breasts. "There. That's better," he announced, seemingly satisfied.

"Gator," she protested, slipping the dress back down where it belonged. "I am not about to go walking around looking like I left my shoulders at home."

He opened his mouth to say something, but the doorbell rang. Watching him yank open the door, she felt a sudden wave of pity for whoever was on the other side. Victoria almost sighed with relief when she saw James.

"Hi, James," Gator growled, throwing her a glare over his shoulder. "Let me give you a hand."

James was juggling a tray of sandwiches. "I think I can manage," he announced. "Just point me toward the kitchen."

"Right through there." Gator pointed with one hand and peeked under the foil that covered the plate with the other. "What kind of sandwiches did you make?" he whispered in her direction, and Victoria noticed another deep crease between his brows. Now what was he frowning about?

"Finger sandwiches," she said, wondering why he was behaving so strangely. She pretended not to notice that he was trying to inch her dress back up over her shoulders.

Her words stopped him cold. "What kind of sandwiches?"

"Finger sandwiches," she repeated. "You know, those little sandwiches with cucumbers, pâté, ham, that sort of thing." She didn't like the look on his face and put her hands on her hips defiantly. "You said not to make anything fancy."

Now he was really scowling. "Let me get this straight. You're going to serve sandwiches filled with cucumbers to forty-five boys who could each eat half a side of beef with room left over for dessert?"

Victoria nodded her head slowly, beginning to see the error of her ways.

Gator rolled his eyes and grabbed her arm, propelling her into motion. "Let's go." He started pulling her toward the front door before she realized what he was up to.

"Wait a minute," she cried, appalled that he was being overbearing again. "We can't go anywhere. You're expecting a houseful of guests."

"Tori, we're going to have some angry guests if we serve those boys your little sandwiches. The boys need food, real food. We'll serve pizza and beer," he announced.

Gator hurried her out the door and down the elevator. The doorman must have had a sixth sense, because Gator's car was parked near the curb and pulled up immediately.

Victoria sat silently in the car as Gator drove. How was she supposed to know that the boys might not like finger sandwiches? She'd never had a party for forty-five football players before. And how was she supposed to know Gator wasn't going to like her dress? Tears welled up in her eyes and she lifted a hand to brush them away.

Up until now, the differences between them had never been a problem. Not really. Even though they came from two separate worlds that, for the moment, seemed only connected because of a silly business deal, Victoria no longer felt there was any difference between them. Not really. When they were together, it was as if they created a world of their own. Until tonight.

"I sure wish you'd say something," he grumbled, glancing at her. "You know I'm not much on small talk."

"I'm sorry about the food." Victoria shrugged her shoulders.

The car swerved and he glared at her for a moment. "Will you stop that!"

"Stop what?" she cried, biting her lip to keep from crying. She had dressed wrong, picked out the wrong food and now he was aggravated with her. Before, his testiness would have made her mad. But for some reason, tonight it only made her sad.

"Stop doing that with your shoulders! Every time you do, that damn dress—" He broke off and muttered under his breath.

"I'm sorry you don't like my dress," Victoria said, turning to look out the window to hide her tears.

"Oh, I like it," he announced, reaching out to pull her closer until she was sitting next to him. She noticed his hand had slipped her dress up on her shoulders again. "That's the problem," he growled, releasing her to shift gears. "I can't stop looking at you. And the boys won't be able to, either." He wheeled around the corner and pulled into the parking lot of Pizza Palace. He shut the car off and turned to her. "Now, we're going to go get some pizza and beer. And you're going to stop shrugging your shoulders and keep that dress up where it belongs. All right?" She couldn't help but notice that the whole time he was complaining about her dress, his eyes kept straying to her bare shoulders and the soft curve of her breasts. It caused a warmth to spread from her stomach to the tip of her toes.

"All right," she agreed, feeling a heavy weight lift from her. She'd rather walk around looking like she'd lost her shoulders somewhere than have Gator mad. Maybe the evening wasn't going to be so bad after all.

She waited for the pizzas while Gator walked next door to buy some beer. Armed with enough food and drinks to serve a small nation, they headed back to the party, which was now in full swing.

No one seemed to have missed them, Victoria realized as she helped serve up slices of the fragrant pizza. Gator poured beer while James swapped recipes with a man large enough to qualify as an office building and who Victoria could only identify as "Cook."

Moving through Gator's spacious apartment, she marveled at the loveliness of it. The rooms were large and spacious, yet decorated beautifully. It would have been easy for an apartment that large to be cold and impersonal, but it wasn't. The color scheme was a mixture of rich and muted blues. Small-print paper covered the walls, while the floors were bare, the wood polished to a high sheen. The furniture was large and inviting. The kitchen was a dream, with every modern appliance. It was also done in shades of blue, an unusual combination in a kitchen, but Victoria found it worked rather well, pulling the apartment together.

Although she was curious, she didn't quite have the nerve to venture down the long hallway that she assumed led to the bedrooms. But she was curious enough to let her mind wander down the hall. She couldn't help but wonder what Gator's bedroom was like.

"Did you get a chance to eat?" She jumped at his voice and whirled to face him, hoping he wouldn't be able to tell she'd just had her mind in his bedroom. He was leaning in the doorway, watching her.

She marveled at the sight of him. She loved looking at him, loved being with him. Loved him. *Loved him,* she thought again, not quite certain her mind was sending out the right signals. But as she stood in the kitchen, watching him, staring at him, she knew without a doubt that yes, she did indeed love him.

He was big and overbearing and at times the most exasperating, irritating human being she had ever encountered. But he was also warm, gentle and wonderful. He had teased and taunted her until she was certain she would cry. But he'd also taught and tempted her and, alas, stolen her heart.

"Tori?" He arched a brow and cocked his head. "Are you all right? This isn't too much for you, is it?"

"No, not at all." Lifting her head, she gave him what she hoped was a bright smile. "I'm fine. I just came in here to grab a few sandwiches. It seemed a shame to waste them." She was mumbling about sandwiches and stalling for time because she didn't know if she could face the fact that she was totally and hopelessly in love with him.

He nodded, his eyes intent on hers. "Why don't you come in and join the party?" he asked softly, while at the same time placing his hands on either side of her face.

She nodded silently and took a long, deep breath. He was telling her something with his eyes, she could sense it. The problem was she just couldn't read the message clearly. The air seemed still around them, and the soft, melodious sound of the tape player wafted in from the living room. Her gaze was pinned to his and her breathing stalled.

"Tori the Terror," he whispered, sliding his hands up and down her cheeks. He gazed deep into her eyes and she worried that he would see the love in them.

"Why don't we go join the party?" she suggested, stepping around him and hoping her steps didn't falter. She needed some time to think, to understand her feelings more clearly.

He nodded and gave her back a little nudge. Pushing through the swinging door, she noticed Spitface and headed toward him. Gator grabbed her arm. "Where are you going?"

"To ask Spitface to dance," she said brightly, wanting to get away from him so she could think.

"You're going to do what!"

She grinned, enjoying the look on his face. "Well, you told me I should get to know the players better. It was your idea." She sashayed away and glided up to Spitface.

"Would you care to dance?" she asked politely.

Spitface blinked furiously and looked around. "With you?" he croaked, and she smiled. Obviously getting involved with her made a lot of people nervous.

"Yes, with me." She sighed as he put his arms around her and stumbled to the music. She couldn't help but compare him to Gator. In looks, there was no comparison. Spitface was blond and fair, and although he was bigger than Gator, he was not nearly as solidly built. And he didn't smell nearly as good. He didn't smell bad; he just didn't smell like Gator.

Getting into the dance a bit more, Spitface's steps seemed steadier as he pulled her a little tighter. His hands splayed her back and she could feel his fingers wiggling upward. She was just about to issue a squawk of protest when she saw a hand clamp down on his shoulder, stopping him in midstep.

"It's going to be mighty hard to play ball with a broken hand." Gator glared at her over the man's shoulder.

"Coach, my hand's not broken."

"No, but it's going to be unless you put it back where it belongs."

"Sorry, coach," he mumbled, giving Victoria a sheepish look before backing away from her. Gator stepped in and gave her such a dark look she almost chuckled. She was suddenly having a wonderful time.

"I think you scared away my dance partner," she teased, slipping her arms around his neck and trying to ignore her body's increased sensitivity at his nearness. She had switched dance partners and her body instinctively knew it, responding immediately to Gator's presence.

"We're even," he muttered, twirling her around and nearly stepping on her toes.

"Even? How's that?" she purred.

"You scared my players," he growled, his breath soft and warm against her ear. "Now I've scared your dance partners. We're even."

"Does this mean you intend to scare the other forty-four players?" she inquired, trying not to grin. She'd found his weak spot and was teasing him unmercifully. She couldn't help it, she loved the idea that he might be jealous.

"It's probably that damn dress," he grumbled, deliberately twirling her to the other end of the living room.

"Gator," she protested, as he pulled her down the hallway that had occupied her thoughts just a few moments before. She had wondered what was down here, but now that she was here, with him, she was nervous. "There's no music in here."

"I know," he said softly, opening the door to a darkened room and pulling her in after him.

"Gator, what are you doing?" He backed her up against the wall. The room was bathed in darkness, but she didn't need light to see his face or his eyes. She could hear what he was feeling in his voice. Her breathing became shallow.

"You want to know what I'm doing, prissy lady?" he asked softly, pressing his hands to the wall on either side of her head and effectively imprisoning her. He gazed down at her and she licked her lips unconsciously. "I'm trying very hard to hang on to my sanity, but you sure as hell are making it difficult for me."

She blinked rapidly. His breath was sweet and danced across her cheeks. He was so close she could see his eyes change and adjust to the darkness. Victoria struggled to hold on to her composure.

"I'm making it difficult? What did I do? I'm not the one whose difficult!" she announced in a huff, forgetting about her dress and throwing her shoulders back.

A tortured groan slipped from his lips and he shook his head. "There you go again, Tori," he ground out, letting his gaze drop to her shoulders before wandering across her breasts. She felt the warmth of his gaze curl her toes. He was so close and she wanted to touch him so badly.

"What?" she asked suddenly.

He sighed deeply and slid his hands slowly up and down her bare shoulders until her skin tingled with delight. "I've been trying very hard," he said in a soft voice. She could feel him strain to hold himself in check. "Very hard, Tori. These past few weeks have been so . . . special." He swore softly and dropped his head. "I'm not very good at this sort of thing."

Victoria smiled inwardly. She had a feeling he was good at everything. Raising a hand to his cheek she gently caressed the rough skin, urging him on.

"I'm not like Rodney," he said softly, letting his fingers find the soft hollow of her neck. Her insides turned to butter and she feared her legs would crumple.

"R-Rodney?" she whispered, wondering what on earth Rodney or whoever had to do with what was happening between them at this moment.

"The guy that wants your house." Gator tangled his fingers through the silky strands of her hair and tipped her head back. Her eyes met his and her breath fled. "Tori, I—I love you."

Her eyes widened and her heart thudded. "Wh-what?" She couldn't believe what she'd just heard him say. She was momentarily speechless, the shock of his words slowly dawning on her.

He hesitated, and for a fraction of a second Victoria feared she had heard him wrong, had only imagined the words she longed to hear.

"I love you, prissy lady. Now, I know I'm not fancy like Rodney, and I know I'm not your type, but sometimes—" He stopped and she knew he was struggling.

"I...I love you, too." She watched the amazement race across his face. "I love you!" Her voice was a muffled whisper as she threw her arms around him.

"You love me?" he repeated, as if he couldn't quite believe it, either.

He loved her! Gator loved her! Her heart spun recklessly. Longing licked up her veins until her mouth ached with need. She lifted her head and her eyes collided with his. Flames of desire ignited within the core of her, and it seemed like an eternity before he bent his mouth to hers.

Hungrily his lips met hers and Victoria wrapped her arms around him, clinging to him. Her body molded to his until she felt every hard inch of him.

His tongue coaxed and nuzzled hers, sizzling her senses until she was spinning helplessly. She gave back everything she got, and wanted more as love squeezed at her heart. Her limbs quivered as the scent of him infiltrated the air she breathed, igniting her with a fire so intense it burned her soul.

Gator's hands slid the length of her, gently caressing her spine, the curve of her hip, the roundness of her bottom. The gentle massage sent currents of desire through every nerve ending. She groaned softly as he pulled her tighter. His lips smothered hers until she was certain she would faint from the pure joy of it.

With a barely muffled groan, he slid his mouth from hers, resting his lips against her cheeks. "Tori, honey, I've tried," he whispered. "I've really tried, but you're driving me crazy." His voice was husky and strained and she found she couldn't concentrate on what he was saying. All she could concentrate on was the intense pounding that roared in her ears.

Victoria didn't want to talk. She wanted his mouth on hers, now and forever. Tangling her fingers through the silky strands of his hair, she pulled his mouth back down over hers and arched closer to him.

Groaning, he took her swollen mouth again and she could feel him shudder as his hand gently moved to caress the soft curve of her breast. The peasant dress was thin, but she could have been wearing nothing for all the protection it afforded from the heat of his hand. His fingers were trembling as he gently caressed her.

Sighing against his mouth, she tried to breathe, but found it near impossible as his hand gently pushed the thin material away from her skin. Dipping his head, his lips traced a molten path until he found what he was seeking.

Gasping, Victoria's head fell back as his mouth moved like velvet across her aching breast, slowly taking possession of her until she grew wild with abandon.

A soft moan filled the room and she realized it came from her. His warm breath against her skin caused her to shiver. Gator trailed his lips upward, planting soft kisses across her awakened skin, softly caressing her everywhere he touched. Finally he found her mouth again. Her lips parted easily as his tongue found hers.

"Coach, we're leaving." The voice echoed down the hall and startled them. Gator pulled his mouth free and uttered a word that turned the dark room blue. Blushing, Victoria pulled her arms to her sides and dropped her head.

"We have to talk," he said softly, adjusting the top of her dress back to its proper position. "But not now, not here." He dropped his lips over hers and for a moment the world stopped. She loved him so. Pulling his mouth free, he gently tapped her nose. "We've got a lot to talk about."

Victoria nodded and wrapped an arm around his waist as he led her out of the room. Her legs barely touched the ground she was so happy. She still couldn't quite believe that Gator loved her.

They bid goodbye to the players and then pitched in to help James clean up. It was well after midnight by the time they had finished.

"I'll go get the car, Victoria." James, sensing they wanted to be alone, left.

"Come here, honey," Gator said as soon as the door shut. She went willingly into his arms, pressing herself against the length of him. This was where she belonged, where she knew she always wanted to be.

Her eyes glowed as he dipped his mouth to hers. She slid her hands up and across his back, savoring the touch of him.

His lips nudged against hers until he felt the sweet recesses of her mouth with his tongue. Victoria sighed happily. Gator loved her. It still didn't seem possible.

"Tori, honey." Gator pulled his mouth from hers and sighed. "You better not keep James waiting." He brushed his lips across her mouth. "I'll talk to you in the morning."

He walked her down to the car, keeping an arm protectively around her waist. There was so much to talk about, so much to say. She didn't really want the evening to end.

"I'll call you," Gator said after he helped her into the car. He leaned in the window and brushed his lips across hers. "I love you, prissy lady," he said, for her ears only.

"I love you, too." She reached out and brushed a fallen curl from his forehead. She didn't want to leave him tonight. There were so many unspoken things.

Gator stood up. "Tomorrow."

Tomorrow, she thought happily. Sighing in contentment, she leaned her head against the seat and closed her eyes.

# *Chapter Eight*

Victoria slowly opened her eyes. Her bedroom was bathed in lemon-splashed sunlight. The warmth filtered through the windows. The drowsy comfort of her bed engulfed her, and with a contented sigh and a smile, she rolled over and pulled the covers to her chin. Gator loved her! She still couldn't believe it. Stretching luxuriously, the reels of her mind began to replay last night's scene. Gator's reaction to her dress, his reaction to Spitface's appreciative glances. Her reactions to his kisses, his caresses. She snuggled deeper. The future suddenly looked bright and promising and full of love. All because of Gator.

The jangling of the telephone brought her out of her thoughts. Lifting herself to her elbow, she picked up the phone, cleared her throat and pressed the receiver to her ear.

"Hello," she murmured.

"Victoria how are you, dear? It's been so long."

She sat upright and pushed a length of her hair out of her face. "William, is that you?"

"Yes, of course, dear. Now tell me, how's my favorite client?"

Victoria smiled. William Browning had been her grandfather's attorney, and now he was hers. But William was more than that, he was also a friend. He had helped cut through all the paperwork and red tape after her grandfather died. And he had tried to cushion the blow when he'd revealed the state of her financial condition.

"I'm fine, William. And you?"

"Wonderful, dear. But I have a feeling you're going to feel much better after I tell you why I'm calling."

Victoria laughed softly. "Unless you're calling to tell me I've won the lottery, or some distant relative I've never met has left me a fortune—"

"Better, dear. Much better. I think I've got a buyer for the Cannons."

"What?" Victoria's heart jumped in her chest and she pressed the phone closer to her ear. "Are you serious, William?" Her mind raced ahead, not quite believing what she was hearing.

"Very serious. I received a call last night from an attorney representing the interested party. I'd like to see you this morning if it's possible. Do you think you can be in my office by ten?"

Grabbing her bedside alarm, Victoria squinted at the numbers. Without her glasses, she couldn't read the broad side of a barn, much less the tiny numerals printed on the face of the clock. "William, what time is it?"

He chuckled softly. "It's eight forty-five. It'll give you plenty of time. The attorney insisted on meeting today, he's coming in this afternoon. But I'd like a chance to talk to you first. From what I gathered, his client is quite interested in closing the deal quickly."

"I'll be there," she assured him, swinging her legs over the side of the bed. "At ten." Hanging up the phone, Victoria bolted out of bed and headed for the shower. A buyer for the Cannons! She couldn't believe it! Finally, the nightmare was over. Finally, she was going to be able to pay off all her bills, get her life together and go forward.

The team and its players would finally be able to get the kind of financial support she hadn't been able to provide. They deserved that much. She would be able to start fresh, with a clean slate, without worrying about the heavy debt hanging over her head.

Victoria grabbed a towel and quickly turned on the faucets. If she hurried, she'd have time to wash and dry her hair and get a cup of coffee into her. She wanted to be wide awake and alert for this meeting. It meant everything.

She hummed happily as the water pelted her, combining with the excitement to wake her up. Suddenly a thought shook her, and she reached out a hand and snapped off the faucets.

A buyer for the Cannons. She groaned softly and shook the water from her hair. Gator! Oh, Lord, in her happiness over the news, she had forgotten what it might mean to him. If the Cannons were sold, he might be out of a job. She knew that occasionally new owners made a stipulation that they be allowed to replace the coaching staff as part of the deal. What if they wanted to buy out Gator's contract? What if he couldn't get another job in football? Her spirits dragged. Although they had made some progress with his image, and the Cannons had won the last few games, that was no guarantee that Gator would be able to get another job. Hadn't he told her that her grandfather had saved his skin?

How could she choose between the man she loved and a team she had to sell? Victoria groaned softly as a heavy weight of despair dropped over her. Why did life have to be so complicated? she wondered. Why couldn't things be a little simpler? For the first time in her life, she was in love. She loved Gator more than anything in the world. How on earth could she hurt him? How could she live with herself? Gator was a man who needed football. It was his life, she'd known that from the beginning. Now, she just might be forcing him out in the cold. How could she do it?

Another thought quickly filled her mind. How would he take the news? she wondered dismally. She'd known right from the beginning he didn't want her to sell the team. Hadn't he asked her to wait a month? She had never realized why before, but now it seemed clear. He must have been worried that if the team was sold, he might be out of a job. Perhaps he'd been trying to line up job offers this past month.

With her thoughts swirling, Victoria sank down on the bed. What on earth was she going to do? She couldn't very well announce to her attorney that she couldn't sell the team because she had fallen hopelessly in love with her head coach. That certainly wouldn't do anybody any good.

Another thought entered her mind and buoyed her spirits. She still owned the team; she could still call some of the shots. She smiled broadly. She would simply tell William that one stipulation of the sale was that they had to keep Gator on as head coach. If not, she wouldn't sell the team. She would point out that Gator had done a wonderful job with the players, was well liked, respected and he got results. Look at how he had turned the Cannons around in just a short period of time. Victoria was certain that, given the chance, Gator could make the Cannons a first-rate team, a team any owner would be proud of. Certainly the new owners couldn't argue with that. Besides, she would also point out that it might be disruptive to hire a new coach mid-season. For the good of the team, it would be best to keep Gator on. If the prospective buyer was really interested in buying the team, he should have no hesitation. She flopped back on the bed, her spirits soaring. Why on earth hadn't she thought of it sooner? She could sell the team and save Gator's job.

The phone rang again, startling her. Victoria bolted upright and snapped up the receiver.

"Hello." Her voice was decidedly cheerful.

"Don't you sound happy this morning." Gator's voice hummed across the telephone lines, warming her heart. She found her smile growing.

"Gator! I'm so glad you called."

"Why?" he chuckled softly. "You don't even know why I'm calling yet. Tori, honey, I've got something to tell you. I tried to tell you—"

"Gator, *I've* got something to tell you. And it can't wait." Had he heard? she wondered. She had to tell him someone was interested in the team—she wanted to tell him first, so that he was prepared. She wanted to assure him his job was secure, she was going to see to it. She rushed on before he could interrupt. "My attorney called this morning. He thinks he's got a buyer for the Cannons. I wanted you to hear it from me first." Taking a deep breath, she plunged forward, praying he would understand. "Gator, I know you don't want me to sell the team. But I really don't have any other choice. You do understand that, don't you?"

"Tori, I have to talk to—"

"I know it's not what you want, but I'm going to make a stipulation in the contract that the new owners have to keep you on. I don't want you to worry about your job." She dropped her voice, aching with love for him. He'd done so much for her, she wanted, needed to do something for him. "Gator, you've done such a marvelous job with the team. I know maybe I haven't told you, but I'm very proud of everything you've done to change the team around. And all you've done for me."

"Tori, is that why you think I don't want you to sell the team? Because you think I'm worried about my job?" His words were strained and she could tell by his voice she had embarrassed him. This was not working out the way she had planned. She would never do anything intentionally to hurt or embarrass him.

"Gator, please, let me finish." It was important for her to get this out in the open. She wanted so much for him to know how much he meant to her. How much she loved him. "Gator, these past few weeks you've taught me so much about life and about people. You're probably the most wonderful thing that ever happened to me. I love you."

"Honey, I love you, too." He sighed deeply. "But I think we have to talk."

Victoria's fingers tightened on the receiver. His voice sounded odd. She could almost imagine the frown that would be creasing his brow. The way his eyes would be darkened. They had a lot to discuss, but maybe now, over the telephone, wasn't the right time. He was a proud man and she knew he would be upset if he thought she was doing this just for him.

"Gator. Please don't worry," she soothed, her voice coming out a soft rush. "We've got a lot of things to discuss, but right now I've got to get dressed for that meeting. Why don't you call me later? I should be done by noon." Victoria held her breath. "I love you. That's all that matters."

"Tori, I love you, too. But there's something I think—"

"Noon, Gator," she repeated softly. She hung up the receiver as if it was on fire. She'd gotten past one hurdle. Now all she had to do was convince the new owners that Gator McCallister had to be kept on. She'd worry about explaining her actions to Gator later. In the long run, she was sure he'd understand. He had to. She loved him.

"Victoria, it's so nice to see you again. It's been much too long." William Browning ushered her into the plush inner sanctuary of his spacious office. As the senior partner of Browning and Newcomb, William had the largest, most deluxe office in the building. Located on the eighth floor, his office had an impressive view of the entire downtown area. "You're looking wonderful, as usual," he commented, as she settled herself comfortably in a leather chair across from his desk.

Victoria smoothed down her skirt. Today, Tori was gone, along with her sweatshirt, jeans and boots. Victoria had taken her place, complete with carefully coiffed chignon, sophisticated pink silk suit and low-heeled pumps. Surprisingly, she felt uncomfortable.

"Well, thank you, William. I can't help but think it has something to do with your news." She smiled affectionately at him.

"Yes, I have to admit I was a bit surprised myself, considering the official announcement hasn't even been made yet. I spent nearly an hour on the phone with the prospective buyer's attorney. I wanted to know how they learned that the Cannons were going to be sold, since it hasn't been announced yet."

Victoria felt a prickling of anxiety dance up her spine. William could be a bit stuffy and old-fashioned at times. She certainly didn't want to discourage a prospective buyer. And she didn't want William to do so either, at least not at this point. Her hands tightened on the armrest of the chair.

"William, you know how rumors fly. It's no secret that I was left nearly penniless when Grandfather died. Obviously selling the team was the only possible solution."

"Yes." He nodded his gray head. "That's what I assumed. I became a bit concerned when the attorney refused to identify his client, though. He claimed his client wanted anonymity, at least for the time being." William's silver brows furrowed in dismay and Victoria struggled to hold on to her patience.

"Does it really matter who the prospective buyer is?" Victoria asked. So what if the prospective buyer wanted to remain anonymous for now? What possible difference could it make? It didn't matter to her; as long as the person had the financial capability to pay for the team, she didn't care who they were.

"Well, it doesn't really matter," William admitted finally. "But there are some rules and regulations we have to adhere to. Then there is the matter of financial backing. Before we enter into any serious negotiations, I want to be sure the people I'm involved with have the funds to execute the deal."

Victoria sighed. She loved William dearly. He had been a good and loyal friend. But if she had to find a buyer that met his approval she might as well forget about selling the team! Not that William wasn't an excellent attorney, he was. But he was also very old money. He was strictly upper-class, and felt duty bound to carry on the traditions set forth by his forefathers. One could say he was zealous about it. Not for the first time did she wonder how her grandfather and William had remained friends for so long. Her grandfather had made his money wildcatting. Jake Fairchild had grown up poor as a church mouse, but once he made his fortune, he had made his way into polite society strictly on the basis of his bank account.

"Go on," she urged, trying to hang on to her patience. She had waited and struggled so long for this moment, she didn't know if she could stand the suspense any longer.

William chuckled softly. "I've got to tell you, Victoria, I was a bit surprised, but it seems your head coach, Gator McCallister, wants to buy the Cannons."

Victoria's eyes popped wide as her head snapped up. The strength drained from her body. Gator? Her Gator? She almost chuckled. There had to be a mistake. Gator McCallister couldn't afford to buy the Cannons. He made a good living as a head coach, but nowhere near what was needed to purchase a professional football team. Not even a second-rate one. There had to be some mistake.

"Are you sure, William?" She leaned forward in her chair and eyed him carefully.

Her attorney nodded. "It took some doing, but his lawyer finally gave me his name. I refused to even discuss a sale unless he divulged his client's name. I didn't want to waste my time or get your hopes up." He smiled gently at her.

"Gator McCallister?" she repeated. "Are you sure?" She heard the tremble in her voice, felt the slow, frantic pace of her heart. The earth seemed to slow on its axis as she waited for William to continue.

"Victoria, are you all right, dear? You look a little peaked." He looked at her carefully and her breathing nearly stopped.

She managed a small smile and prayed there had been a mistake. This couldn't be possible. Gator. Her Gator couldn't be interested in buying the Cannons. Surely he would have mentioned something to her. Waves of trepidation rolled over her.

"I'm fine," she lied, her voice low and controlled. "Now tell me more about this deal. Are you sure it's the same Gator McCallister that's the head coach of the Cannons?" She frowned. "Where on earth would he get the money to buy a professional football team?"

William nodded. "Yes, I'm quite certain it's the same man. I ran a very careful check on him. Apparently Gator McCallister's real name is Martin McCallister. He comes from a very old-line Philadelphia family, strictly social register. The fact that he discarded that life-style years ago hasn't hampered his bank balance any. Seems he inherited millions when he turned twenty-one.'' William shook his head. ''You know, I was just as stunned as you are. When your grandfather hired him as a coach, I wanted to do a basic check into his background, but your grandfather was adamant. He didn't want me poking into McCallister's background. For the life of me I couldn't understand why.'' William smiled affectionately. ''I have to admit, I'm very impressed. I never once connected Gator McCallister with the McCallisters of Philadelphia. It simply never occurred to me that there was a connection. We're talking about a very, very wealthy man, Victoria. He has the resources not only to buy the Cannons, but also to infuse the team with some real money and perhaps make it a first-class team. You couldn't ask for a more financially suitable buyer. Not to mention the fact that Mr. McCallister has an abundance of knowledge about the team and the sport. It's really very wonderful for everyone concerned. He's an absolutely first-rate candidate to buy the team.''

Victoria's mouth went dry and her fingers tightened on the armrests. She was trying to digest all of the information William had supplied her with, but it was hard. All she could think about was the fact that Gator McCallister was rich. Rich! She was reeling in shock. He'd never given her any indication—never even hinted that he was wealthy. Her thoughts raced. She had wondered about all the money they had spent buying new clothes. And what was it that he said? Her lids lowered as she tried to remember. Something about letting her know when he got down to his last few million? At the time she was certain he was joking. Now she realized dismally that he had been telling her the truth. Gator was worth millions. Why hadn't he told her? Why had he pretended to be something he wasn't? A cold dose of suspicion washed over her and Victoria leaned back in her chair for support, afraid she might topple if she didn't.

"How much?" she asked weakly, wondering at what price fools were going today.

"Excuse me?" William was looking at her strangely.

"How much did he offer?" Her nerves were frozen and she clenched her jaw tightly to keep it from clattering. She was suddenly cold, colder than she had ever been in her life.

"Victoria, we really haven't gotten around to talking price, yet. I thought it best to talk to you first. I'm sure that we'll be able to extract a fair price. After all, he seems quite willing, not to mention anxious to purchase the Cannons. He has hands-on knowledge of the inner workings of this particular team, that's certainly in our favor."

She nodded her head, unable to get any words past the lump in her throat. Hands-on knowledge. Victoria winced inwardly. The team wasn't the only thing Gator had hands-on knowledge of. Shame suffused her cheeks.

"Victoria," William went on gently. "The Cannons aren't exactly a big money-maker, you know that yourself. With the amount of revenue going out to the stadium, the park district, plus payroll and other expenses, we should seriously consider any fair offers. With the team's record and the expense factor involved, I'd say that we should take this deal, if the money is right. You're certainly not in any position to continue to support the team. I think we should consider any serious offers. Who knows how long it might be before we get another one."

She'd heard enough. While her mind tried to deny it, her heart knew the truth. Victoria stood up abruptly. "William, please don't make any commitments until you hear from me."

"Victoria?" William stood up and rounded his desk. He put a hand on her shoulder. "Are you sure you're all right?"

She looked at him blankly. She was quite certain she would never be all right again. Numbness gathered around her like a familiar shawl and she nodded, scarcely aware of her action. "I guess selling the team was a bit more traumatic than I expected." William smiled in understanding and patted her shoulder.

"You go on home and think about it. I won't make any commitments until I hear from you. I'm sure I can stall for a day or two, but not much longer."

Biting her lip to keep from crying out, Victoria nodded and rushed toward the door, praying she could hold on to her emotions until she got home.

Fury and sorrow engulfed her. Gator McCallister, her Gator McCallister, was really Martin McCallister, the man who wanted to buy her football team.

Victoria drove blindly through the streets, her mind reeling in shock. Gator had lied to her and betrayed her, but worst of all, he had broken her heart.

She let herself into the house and expelled a sigh of relief when she realized James was out. She rushed to her bedroom, kicked off her shoes and threw herself across her bed, refusing to cry. She was going to handle this with ladylike dignity. She had to put the puzzle pieces together.

Gator McCallister wanted the Cannons. There was no use pretending there was some mistake. Martin McCallister and Gator McCallister were one and the same.

Why hadn't he told her he was rich? Why had he pretended to be something he wasn't? And why hadn't he told her he wanted the Cannons for himself? The reality of the situation struck her like a hammer and she cried out in anguish. It was all very clear now.

Victoria sat up abruptly as the fog in her mind began to clear. Her heart shattered into a million tiny bits as the puzzle pieces began to slip quickly into place. She finally knew what Gator McCallister was going to get out of the deal.

## *Chapter Nine*

Pressing her hands to her eyes, she sought to squelch the thoughts that tortured her soul. It was no use. She knew the truth.

Gator had lied to her and betrayed her, but worst of all he had used her and broken her heart. He was no different than Roger Malcolm, she realized, feeling the icy pangs of defeat tug at her soul. But at least Roger had been honest about what he was. He had readily admitted he wanted her house. Roger had made no pretense about it.

Gator McCallister, on the other hand, had never so much as uttered a word about wanting her football team for himself. He was no different than anyone else. She had something he wanted. The team. What a fool she had been! Why hadn't she questioned his motives when he'd told her he'd help her? Why on earth had she been so naive to believe that Gator was doing it simply to pay back her grandfather?

Because, her mind screamed, she had been so caught up in her own problems and in her own reaction to the man's physical presence that she hadn't bothered to consider that Gator wasn't exactly what he appeared to be. She had let her overactive hormones rule her mind and her heart. She had never bothered to "look below the surface," as Gator would say. Now she knew it was a grave mistake. There was a lot more to Martin "Gator" McCallister below the surface.

Dawning horror forced her eyes closed and Victoria tried to pretend the worst hadn't happened. But it had.

He had pretended to be something he wasn't. He had pretended he was interested in her, pretended he was in love with her, when he wasn't. He was only using her to get what he wanted. He couldn't possibly have any real feeling for her and do what he had done.

How long had he intended to keep up the charade? she wondered. Until she signed on the dotted line? Until she handed the Cannons over to him? Hysterical laughter welled up inside of her. Just this morning she had been concerned about hurting him and his pride. She had worried about him losing his job! Little did she know that a few hours later she would be the one who would be hurt.

Now she understood why he wanted her to wait a month to sell the team. He didn't want her selling it to anyone but him. He wanted a chance to buy the team before any official announcement of the impending sale was made. He had a direct lead to everything that was going on. Anguish squeezed her heart and Victoria bolted upright.

Improve his image! She winced. Martin Gator McCallister must have had a laugh or two over that one. Old-line Philadelphia family, socially prominent! She snorted in disgust. What an absolute fool! She'd been walking around trying to teach him a few things about etiquette, manners and the proper way to dress when all the time he probably could have taught her a thing or two! She sighed bitterly and gave in to the sobs that tore through her.

Each tear seemed to widen the cracks in her shattered heart. Why had he done this to her? Why? Crying until there wasn't a tear left in her eyes, or an ounce of strength in her body, Victoria wiped her swollen eyes, blew her nose and marched to the bathroom to wash her face.

Squaring her shoulders, she forced herself to look in the mirror. She had been a fool. A blind, trusting fool. But what was done was done, and there wasn't anything she could do about it now. Gator had used her, lied to her and betrayed her. But she was still the owner of the Chicago Cannons football team. She'd starve before she turned the team over to him!

With grim determination, Victoria made up her mind to do something. But what? Her eyes moved around the room, finally settling on the green sweatshirt Gator had bought her the first day they had gone shopping. It was hanging in her closet, along with the other sweatshirts she had accumulated in the past few weeks.

Head high, Victoria marched across the room and ripped the shirt off the hanger. Never, ever again would she forget who she was. She was Victoria Louise Fairchild, not Tori, the figment of Gator's, or should she say Martin's, imagination.

"Victoria Louise Fairchild!" she repeated, her voice cold with fury. Grabbing her scissors, she cut the sweatshirt into shreds, hoping for some relief from the pain tearing at her heart. But the sight of the torn and tattered garment only caused another spurt of tears and she sank to the ground, cradling the shirt in her arms. "Gator," she whispered, sobbing uncontrollably. "How could you do this to me?"

"Victoria? Where are you?" James's voice filtered up the stairway, startling her. Jumping up, she quickly hid the torn remnants of her sweatshirt in the back of her closet. There was no point in upsetting James with her problems. Not yet, anyway. He'd know soon enough.

"I'm in my room, James," she called, wiping her nose and trying to school her face into a controlled mask. She cast a quick glance in the mirror and frowned at her reflection. Her eyes were red and swollen and her skin was blotchy. Why couldn't she cry with some dignity? she wondered. Why did she always end up looking like a shriveled tomato?

"The coach called a little bit ago. He said he'd call back. He was real disappointed he missed you, and told me to give you his love." James smiled and Victoria scowled.

"His love," she mocked, not caring that James was looking at her like she'd lost her mind. "How touching. Was there anything else he wanted to give me? Perhaps a few more lies?"

"Victoria, what on earth has gotten into you?" James stepped into the room and looked at her closely. "Have you been crying?"

"No," she lied, turning from his inspection. "I haven't been crying. I've been wising up. It's quite an experience." She couldn't help it, her voice broke and another round of tears filled her eyes.

"I don't know what's going on, but I'm going down to make you a strong cup of tea. You come down and tell me what's troubling you." He turned and walked out the door. Victoria opened her mouth to protest. She didn't feel like talking to anyone at the moment. Didn't feel like admitting what a fool she'd been. All she wanted to do was crawl in a hole and hide her shame.

"And don't go giving me any of your lip," James cautioned over his shoulder before she could voice the words. "I didn't fancy it when you were a child and I'm not about to now. You just go wash your face and bring yourself down these stairs. Now." It wasn't a request, but a command, and Victoria knew there was no point in arguing with him.

A weak smile lifted her lips. What on earth would she have done without James? He was the only person she could trust. The only person who truly loved her for what she was, and not for what she had. He had stuck by her during the worst times. Right now, she wondered if the worst times were yet ahead of her.

Obediently, she followed him down the stairs, trying to quell the sudden rush of tears that kept pooling in her eyes. She had to stop crying. She had to stop feeling sorry for herself. She had to... handle the situation.

"Now, what is it that's making you so unhappy?" James dropped two cups to the table with a clatter and motioned her to sit down. "I haven't seen you looking this unhappy since your grandpa died."

Victoria dropped wearily into the chair. Maybe she would feel better if she told someone. Not that James could change the facts. Nothing could alter what she had learned, but somehow, James always managed to make things better.

"I went to see William Browning today." She lifted her gaze to his. James's face was impassive as he waited for her to continue. "He told me that Gator wants to buy the Cannons."

"That's wonderful!" James burst out, thumping the table with his hand. "That's the best news we've had in ages. It's got to set your mind at ease knowing the team's going to be with such a fine man."

Appalled, Victoria gaped at him in shock. What on earth was in the tea he was drinking? "Wonderful!" she exploded. "That man's not wonderful and neither is the news! Gator McCallister's real name is Martin, and he lied to me and used me. He only pretended to be interested in me so he could get his hands on the team." A sob burst loose and Victoria buried her head in her hands. Telling James was supposed to make her feel better. She suddenly felt worse.

James's eyes widened and he shook his head. "I don't know whose been filling your mind with these lies, but Gator isn't like that. He cares for you, Victoria, he really does. And if he wants to buy the team, I don't see what one has to do with the other." He shook his head and Victoria realized James really didn't understand.

"He's rich!" she exploded. "And he pretended to be something he's not. If his intentions were honorable—"

James's hand flew up in the air to halt her words. "Wait a minute. Just because he never told you what his bank balance is doesn't mean he lied to you. Did you ever ask him how much money he had?" He watched her expectantly, waiting for an answer.

"Well, no, of course not," she admitted reluctantly. "It never seemed to matter. It simply never occurred to me that—"

"I see." James nodded. "Just because you thought, because you assumed that the coach didn't have any money, that means the man lied to you? Am I hearing you correctly?" She hadn't heard that tone of voice or seen that frown on his face since she was seven years old and had cut all the flowers off his prize-winning rosebush.

Victoria sighed. When James put it like that, she had to admit it didn't actually seem like Gator lied to her. But why hadn't he told her he was rich? Why had he pretended to be something he wasn't? He must have had a reason.

"James," she returned, trying to read his face. "Gator could have told me he was rich."

He sniffed haughtily. "Why? What difference does it make? I don't remember it being a law that you have to tell a woman you're rich before you fall in love with her." His brown eyes impaled her and Victoria shifted nervously. She had always assumed that James would be on her side. Now, she wasn't so sure. James had always been the one person she could turn to, no matter what. The one person she could always count on to back her up, to take her side. Was he so enamored with Gator that he couldn't see the man clearly, either? She really couldn't blame him. She, too, had been taken in.

"Victoria, I thought I brought you up to be a fair and compassionate person. It's not like you to go jumping to conclusions. You owe Gator a chance to explain. I think you should sit down and talk to him about this. You've come to a lot of vicious conclusions without giving the man a chance to defend himself. That's not right." He sighed softly. "You owe it to him, and to yourself. You love him, and he loves you. Don't let something like a misunderstanding come between you."

"Misunderstanding?" Victoria echoed in shock. Her heart was broken, her life destroyed and James thought it was a misunderstanding! "I don't think I owe him anything. What possible explanation can Gator have for lying to me?"

James stood up and swept the cups from the table, dropping them into the sink with a clatter. "You won't know until you talk to him. Now he said he'd call back. When he does, talk to him. Ask him about all this. I'm sure he'll have a logical explanation. You'll see." James filled the sink with soapy water and began to wash the cups. It was clear the conversation was over. Victoria stood up, her thoughts spinning.

"Are you going to talk to him when he calls?" James asked, turning to her.

For a moment, she hesitated, then finally she nodded her head. "I'll talk to him." What she had to say would only take a few minutes, she decided as she went back up to her room. She would know in just a few minutes if there had been a misunderstanding, or if Gator had deliberately lied and misled her.

Victoria paced her room, waiting for Gator's call. He had told James he would call later, but how much later? It was almost six in the evening and she had told him she'd be back by noon. Why hadn't he called? Was it because he no longer needed to keep up the facade anymore? He no longer needed to pretend to be interested in her.

The thought brought a decided ache to her heart. Maybe, like the old saying, she couldn't see the forest for the trees. Maybe she didn't want to admit she could be such a fool.

The ringing of the phone jarred her. Victoria jumped and reached out a hand to grab the receiver.

"Hello."

"Tori, honey."

"Gator, is that you?"

"Yes, honey." He sounded tired and for a moment her resolve faltered.

"Gator, I have to talk to you," she blurted, not waiting for him to explain why he was calling so late. "Are you rich?"

"What?" The word exploded through the phone and she cringed. She'd forgotten how powerful his voice was. Even across the miles of telephone wires she could feel the impact rock her. "What the hell kind of a question is that? What happened to 'how are you?' Are you all right? Is anything wrong?" His voice had grown sharper, but she decided to ignore it.

"Gator, or should I say *Martin*?" Even to her own ears her voice sounded unnaturally high. "Please, just answer the question," she snapped, unable to keep the bitterness out of her voice.

"What the hell's gotten into you?" he barked. Victoria winced.

"The only thing that's gotten into me is sense," she replied coolly. "Common sense. Gator, why won't you answer my question? What have you got to hide?" She heard his quick intake of breath.

"Hide! Woman! Have you been drinking?" he bellowed, and she pulled the phone away from her ear. He wasn't mad. He was furious. "Tori, I think you have a problem here and I'm not sure I understand. Maybe you'd better explain yourself."

"The name is Victoria," she said quietly. "Victoria Louise Fairchild. And you're the one who needs to do the explaining, not me. Under the circumstances, I think the least you can do is give me an honest answer. I deserve that much." She held her breath and prayed she wouldn't cry. She didn't want to give him the satisfaction of knowing how hurt she was.

"Honest!" he exploded. "I've never been anything but honest with you, Victoria." He drew her name out slowly, and she cringed. Somehow coming from him, "Victoria" sounded strange. She'd always been Tori.

"Why didn't you tell me?" There was a long silence on the other end and she feared he had hung up. "Gator?"

"Why didn't I tell you what? That I was rich? I didn't tell you," he said, his voice deadly cold, "because I didn't think it mattered. I thought for once you might be able to look below the surface of things and see what really mattered." He gave a disgusted snort. "I guess I was wrong. If I had known it was important, I would have told you. Yes, to answer your question, I'm rich. As a matter of fact, Victoria Louise Fairchild, I'm filthy, stinking rich."

His words echoed through her brain. She swallowed hard and tried hard to hang on to what little composure she had left. Her eyes burned with tears, but she swallowed them back; she wasn't going to cry.

"Why didn't you just tell me the truth from the beginning? Why did you lie to me? Why did you pretend to be something you weren't? And what was all that about repaying a debt to my grandfather?" She laughed harshly, knowing she was on the verge of hysteria. She knew she couldn't hold back the tears much longer.

"Tori, I thought you were different. I thought you were something special. I thought I had finally gotten through to you. That first day at the football field, you thought I was one thing. But just because that's what you thought I was didn't make it so. And right now, you're thinking one thing about me, but honey, let me tell you something, just thinking it doesn't make it so." He paused as she tried to pay attention to his words and not to the pressure that was squeezing her heart.

"Sure I'm rich. So what? I didn't think it mattered to you how much money I had. You never asked me about it. If you would have, I'd've told you. You just assumed I didn't have any money."

"Is it true that you want to buy the team?" A heavy hand squeezed her heart as she waited for his answer.

"It's true."

She sighed deeply. "You know, Gator, I thought *you* were different. But you're just like everyone else. You wanted something from me. You wanted the team. Why didn't you just tell me that in the beginning? You're no better than Roger." She paused to take a deep breath. "Mr. McCallister," she said crisply, gathering her courage. "The Chicago Cannons football team is not for sale. Not to you. Not at any price. Not ever!" Slowly, and with deliberate care, Victoria hung up the phone.

# *Chapter Ten*

For long, silent moments, Victoria sat with her hand on the receiver. An unexpected shiver shook her frame and she wrapped her arms around herself, struggling to breathe past the lump in her throat. Dawning horror paralyzed her. The pain in her heart ached to the depths of her soul.

There was a gentle tap at her door and she pulled herself together as best she could. "Come in." Her voice was hoarse and teary and she prayed James wouldn't notice.

"Was that Gator?" Dressed in his coat, James stood in the doorway looking at her.

She lifted her eyes to his and nodded dully, not trusting herself to speak.

"Did you get things straightened out?"

She nodded again and hoped her voice didn't betray her anguish. "I found out everything I needed to know," she said softly. Eyeing him skeptically, she asked, "Where are you going?"

"To the movies with Mrs. Begner." At the slight inclination of her brow he continued. "You know, the widow who moved in next door." He frowned and stepped into the room. Victoria tried to keep a tight rein on her feelings, wanting to hide her shame. This was one thing James couldn't protect her from. This she had to handle all on her own.

"How long have you been seeing Mrs. Begner?" she asked, hoping it would stop any further questions about Gator.

James ignored her. "Are you sure you're going to be all right? Maybe I'll just stay home. You look like you could use some company." James stepped into the room and started to pull off his coat.

Drawing a deep breath, Victoria managed a weak smile. "I'll be fine, James. You go on and don't worry about me. It's been a long day and I'm tired. I think I'll just take a shower and go to bed." She forced her lips into a smile. "Really, go on now," she insisted, forcing her smile wider. "I can take care of myself."

James looked at her for a long moment, opened his mouth to say something, then snapped it shut. Turning, he shut the door softly behind him.

Victoria sat motionless on the bed, unwilling and unable to move her body. Her happiness, her joy, had been brushed away like cobwebs by Gator's words. How could Gator have done this? she wondered, swallowing the lump in her throat.

She shook her head, as if trying to shake the hurt away. Misery was suffocating, she decided, as she peeled off her clothes. She would take a shower and then go to bed. There was nothing else she could do tonight. Tomorrow would be soon enough to think of what had to be done. She still had a team to sell. But she couldn't think about it tonight, she reasoned, as she headed for the bathroom. She couldn't think about that quite yet.

A mournful sigh lifted her shoulders as she stepped under the pulsating water. If only the water could wash away her pain, she thought, tipping her head back. She wouldn't cry, she told herself. She simply wouldn't!

The doorbell rang and Victoria cursed softly. James must have forgotten something. Quickly throwing her robe over her damp body, she hurried down the stairs and opened the door. Her eyes widened. It wasn't James—it was Gator. She gasped.

"What are you doing here?" she demanded, glaring up at him.

He shouldered his way into the house without waiting for an invitation. "We have to talk."

Shivering, she drew herself up and pulled the robe tighter around her. "We don't have anything to talk about. Now, I'd appreciate it if you would leave." She mentally willed him to go. He didn't seem the least bit affected by her words or her glare.

His eyes touched her face, the wet strands of her hair, the soft curves outlined by the terry-cloth robe. Victoria's heart began to pound, but she tried to ignore it.

"I'm not going anywhere until we talk," he announced.

"Suit yourself," she replied in a huff. "You can stand here all night for all I care." She spun on her heel and charged up the stairs.

"Tori!" he growled.

Victoria heard him on the steps behind her and quickened her pace. She wasn't even decent, for heaven's sake! Rushing into her room, she deliberately slammed the door in his angry face, feeling an immense surge of satisfaction.

"Go away!" she called, her heart pounding.

"If you don't open this door, I'm going to break it down."

She didn't doubt for a moment he would do exactly that! Victoria groaned. She wasn't up to this. She wasn't up to seeing him or talking to him. What she needed was some time to compose herself. She doubted if she'd ever get over her love for him, doubted that she'd ever be able to look at him or see him without it having a profound effect on her. Maybe in time she would be able to face him coolly and confidently, knowing she wouldn't break into tears. But not just yet.

"Please, Gator," she pleaded, her voice choked with emotion. "Just go away." She rested her head against the door. Maybe tomorrow she would be strong enough to look at him and not melt. Maybe tomorrow she could be in his presence and not ache with love for him. And maybe tomorrow the sun wouldn't rise, she thought dully.

"Is that what you really want, Tori?" he asked quietly.

Victoria sighed in frustration. What she really wanted was to go back to last night when she was happy. When she thought Gator loved her. But she knew it was not possible.

"Yes," she said softly, knowing as she said the word it was the final blow on whatever they had shared.

He sighed heavily. "All right. If that's what you really want." There was a moment of silence and Victoria's heart struggled with her mind. She didn't want him to go, but she couldn't find the strength to stop him. She had some pride left.

"Goodbye, prissy lady," he said softly, giving the door a gentle tap. "I love you. Take care of yourself."

The tears finally came. It took all her self-control not to rip the door open and stop him. But she couldn't. She loved him as she would never love anyone else, but it would never work. He had lied to her and used her, and she just couldn't forget it.

Victoria sank to the floor, letting the sobs overtake her. She cried until there were no tears left. Gator was gone from her life forever. It was over. It was hard to believe, but it was true. The knowledge left a decided ache in the depths of her soul.

Wiping her eyes, she opened her bedroom door. She wanted to bolt the front door, just in case he decided to return. Barefoot, she padded down the hall.

"Gotcha!" Gator's voice pierced the darkness and she screamed as his arms tightened around her waist.

"You tricked me!" she yelled, as he swept her up and threw her over his shoulder. She swung impotently at him, but he ignored her. Impervious to her flying fists, Gator stomped into her bedroom and dumped her on the bed.

"You tricked me!" she repeated again, scooting backward on the bed and trying to keep her robe closed at the same time.

"I sure did," he announced without the least bit of remorse. "Now, you're going to sit there until you tell me what the hell's going on! And I don't care if it takes all night." Hands on his hips, he stood over her.

"I'm not going to tell you anything!" she snapped, glaring at him.

"And why not?"

"Because," she shot back, aware that his eyes were roaming across her in a way that was making her extremely...warm. She tried to ignore the heat that spread from the tips of her toes upward to touch every female nerve ending until she nearly screamed with awareness. Her thoughts scattered in a million directions as his eyes settled finally on the soft curve of her breast, which was spilling out of the opening of the robe. "B-because...I'm not dressed."

"Well then, get dressed, woman!"

She gave her head a toss, forgetting to grasp the robe, which slipped open more with each movement. "I won't!" she cried petulantly. He was not ever going to overwhelm her again. Victoria swallowed. She hoped.

"Have it your way, then. If you won't get dressed, then I'll have to get undressed." He reached up and slowly began to unbutton his shirt. Her eyes widened and her heart stopped. Was the man crazy? What on earth was he doing? She watched in stunned disbelief as he leisurely drew his shirt off. Wide-eyed, she stared at the broad expanse of his shoulders, the muscles rippling along his arms. A faint dusting of dark hair matted his wide chest, narrowing down to a V at the top of his jeans. Her breathing stopped when he reached down and unsnapped his pants. Lord, he wouldn't dare, would he? For a brief, frantic moment, all Victoria could do was stare at the magnificence of his body. Pulling her eyes from him, she struggled to find her voice.

"Wh-what are you doing?" She forced herself to meet and hold his steady gaze, despite what it was doing to her. The rugged physical presence of the man radiated through her and she struggled to keep her attention on the matters at hand.

He stopped abruptly, his hand poised on his zipper. She tried to harness her reeling senses as his eyes met hers. "Well, you said you couldn't talk to me because you're not dressed. Since you're uncomfortable without your clothes on, the least I can do is take mine off. I'm a gentleman," he said, with a great deal more emphasis than necessary. "And I certainly wouldn't want you to be uncomfortable." His hand moved to his zipper again and she muttered a few colorful words under her breath. He stopped abruptly and tried to look properly shocked.

"Tori," he said, shaking a finger at her and struggling not to grin. "It's not polite to cuss. Ladies do not cuss."

The urge to hit him was so strong she clenched her fists tightly into balls. "What are you doing here?"

"Taking my clothes off," he returned pleasantly, bending down to tug off his boots. She'd had enough. Victoria scooted forward on the bed.

"All right!" she cried, attempting to stand and keep the robe covering all the necessary parts at the same time.

He grabbed her around the waist and tackled her to the bed, landing squarely on top of her.

"Oh, no you don't," he growled. "I'm not that stupid, despite the fact that I might look it. I know damn well the minute you get up you're going to make a run for it and slam some more doors in my face. You're not leaving this room, this bed, dressed or not, until we talk." His eyes met hers and she could feel the warmth of his breath on her neck, sending a bouquet of shivers up and down her. Goose bumps rose like blisters across her bare skin. She swallowed hard. Lord, he was so handsome. Did he have to smell so good, too? How much was she expected to endure?

"Get off of me!" Her first impulse was acute rage and she pummeled his bare chest with her fists, her anger giving her added strength.

"Tori!" he scolded, grabbing her hands and pinning them over her head. "Ladies do not hit people. It's really not polite." He smiled tenderly and she wanted to smack him again.

"I'll give you polite!" she threatened, anger narrowing her eyes. Grunting, she tried to push him off her.

Completely ignoring her near-naked state, Gator lounged indolently on top of her, settling himself comfortably. She decided she was going to keep up a cool, composed front. Even if it killed her!

"Now, Tori, the way I figure it, we can do this the easy way or the hard way, but believe me, we're gonna do it! We're going to talk! Do you understand?"

She blinked back tears. The words hung in the air between them, heavy and foreboding, reminding her of what he had done. Tears pooled in her eyes and her face crumpled. "You're rich," she blubbered, sniffling hard.

"Well, honey, I didn't think being rich was anything to cry about." Lifting a hand, he brushed a thumb across her cheek to wipe her fallen tears. "If I knew it was important to you, I would have told you a long time ago. I didn't think you cared about money."

The way he said it made her cringe. She didn't care a twit about his money, or how much he had of it. What she cared about was what he planned to do with it. Buy the Cannons. *Her* Cannons.

"I don't!" she cried breathlessly, clutching the bedspread and trying to free herself from his hold. "But I thought—I just assumed—how come you didn't tell me?" Eyes wide, she looked at him. What was it in his eyes? she wondered. If she didn't know better, she'd swear it was love shining in their dark depths.

"Honey, it just never seemed important. I don't run around shouting, I'm rich! I'm rich! That certainly wouldn't be very polite." He grinned devilishly and she found a smile tugging at her mouth. She had to admit, Gator always made her smile. Always made her laugh. Tears welled up in her eyes again.

"Why didn't you tell me you wanted to buy the Cannons?" She blinked and looked away, not wanting him to see the pain in her eyes. She could feel the moistness of her tears on her lashes. He bent his mouth to kiss her tears away. She was visibly touched, but tried to ignore it. She wasn't going to let him kiss away or caress away her fears.

He shifted the lower portion of his body until he fit snugly against her. She noticed his breathing was becoming more ragged with each passing moment. The robe was dangerously loose over her breasts and high on her hips. Victoria tried to stay still as her breasts thrust recklessly against the ever-widening gap in the material.

"Well, if you would have asked me right out this afternoon, I would have explained. Now, if you promise to lay still—" His voice broke and he groaned softly as he shifted his frame against her. She couldn't ignore the fact that there was nothing between them except a thin, terry-cloth robe and his jeans and enough electricity to light up the entire state.

"I don't know how much longer I'm going to be able to stay in this position and hang on to my sanity. You're driving me crazy, honey."

"Me!" she cried, forgetting his words and trying to sit up. All she succeeded in doing was molding herself more closely to him. His warm weight pressed against her and she noticed his breathing was labored. The soft material of his jeans caressed her thighs as his legs rubbed against hers. Groaning softly, Gator buried his face in her neck. His breath was sweet and warm, sending her heart into spasms.

Sighing deeply, he lifted his head, his look tortured. "Now, not a word until I'm finished. Promise?"

She opened her mouth, then quickly snapped it shut as his brows rose.

*"Still,"* he emphasized, lifting his finger to her lips to silence any words she might issue. "Now, here it is as quick as I can. Yes, I'm rich. I didn't tell you because I didn't know it was important. I didn't think money mattered to you." His words were rushed and jagged and she could tell from his response that he was having a hard time concentrating on what he was saying.

"Gator, why don't we get up?" She blushed and tried to wiggle out from under him, but there was no escaping the heat or male presence of his body. "It might be a bit easier for both of us."

He shook his head. "I'm not going anywhere until we get this settled. I'm where I belong, Tori," he said softly, and tears welled up in her eyes again. "And I'm not moving until I convince you. I thought what I was doing was right, but this afternoon, on the phone, I realized I'd made a big mistake. Do you remember the first day you came to the field? The day you jammed your finger in my chest and told me I needed a distemper shot?" He lifted her hand off the bed and tenderly kissed the tips of each of her fingers, the ones she remembered she had jammed into his chest.

Victoria nodded, not quite sure what he was getting at. "I remember."

"I think I fell in love with you that moment." Her eyes widened. "Tori, when I came to the house that first day, after you fired me, I came here to offer to buy the team. I knew I had fallen for you like a ton of bricks. I wanted you and the team. But when I found you with that Rodney guy, and you told me he wanted your house and your body, well, I was afraid if I told you I wanted to buy the Cannons you'd think I was just like him. You told me that everyone wanted something from you. Hell, I wanted you, too, but not like that Rodney guy."

"Roger," she corrected, lifting a hand to touch his cheek. He pressed his face against the softness of her hand. Her heart tripped frantically until she feared he could detect the movement beneath the robe.

"Whatever! I guess I just didn't go about this in the right way. You might say I did this kinda as—well, let's just say I did this backward. But I was so in love with you from the moment I laid eyes on you I couldn't think straight. You were just so prim and proper I didn't know what to do or how to act. I figured if I bought the Cannons from you *before* I asked you to marry me, you'd know I loved you for yourself and not because of the damn team." He grinned sheepishly. "Hell, if I owned the team already, you'd have to know I loved you for you, and not for what you had."

"Marry you?" she repeated in disbelief. "You were going to ask me to marry you?" Victoria stared up at him, her heart filled with love.

"Well," he admitted with a wicked grin. "I really wasn't going to *ask*. I was sort of just going to order you to, or else."

"Or else what?" She smiled happily and deliberately shifted her frame.

"Woman! Please," he growled in a tortured whisper. "Stay still! You're driving me crazy." He tried to shift his weight off her, but Victoria slipped her arms around him and held him in place.

"Crazy, huh?" She smiled up at him, thrilled and a bit tortured herself. He was having the same effect on her as she was having on him. "But why did you agree to let me improve your image?"

Ducking his head, he grinned. "I was afraid you wouldn't be interested in someone like me. That's why I asked you to wait a month to sell the team. I figured in a month, being such a lady, you'd be able to improve my image enough so that you wouldn't be embarrassed to marry me. That's why I kept telling you to look below the surface of things. I figured if you got to know me a little better, if you looked below the surface maybe you'd see I was an all-right guy."

She gaped at him in shock. Didn't he know she could never be embarrassed about him? She loved him. She adored him. He was the warmest, kindest, most generous human being she had ever met. How on earth could he even imagine such a thing?

"Gator," she said softly, her heart filled with love. "I could never—" He pressed a finger to her lips to silence her.

"Now, I know I'm not fancy like Roger, and I don't have his highfalutin ways." Gator shook his head. "I tried telling you last night." He grinned. "Last night I had other things on my mind." His eyes raked over her, caressing her face, the hollow of her neck, the curve of her breasts spilling out from the robe.

"When you pulled me down the hall and we—"

He nodded, letting his hands explore the silkiness of her neck, her shoulders. "I just couldn't seem to get my mind to work. That's become a habit when you're around." He moved and groaned and she laughed softly. "I love you. I'm rich. And I want to buy the team. Not for any other reason except I wanted you to know that I loved you for yourself and wanted to marry you for *you*, and not for the damn team, or anything else you had. Now, before I lose my self-control and do something that might shock a lady like you, give me your answer. Will you marry me?" He looked down at her. His eyes were so hopeful, so expectant, she laughed.

"Yes, I will marry you."

"Oh, Tori." Ruthlessly he pressed his body against hers until she moaned with desire. His lips took hers with an urgency that excited her. She responded eagerly, love erasing all doubts, all hurt. She lifted her hands to his bare shoulders, allowing her fingers the pleasure of him.

Her breasts strained against the terry cloth as his touch turned her skin to liquid fire, burning and searing her to him. Victoria moaned. Adrenaline flooded in her veins until she was dizzy and breathless. The weight of his thighs caressed her, the material of his pants a sensual barrier that only heightened her awareness. The male scent of him dizzied her and she moved against him.

"Tori." His breath was ragged as he pulled his mouth free. "I love you."

"I love you, too."

He sighed in relief. "Good! Then let's go, woman!" Gator rolled off the bed and scooped her up in his arms.

"Go?" she asked, wondering what the hurry was. "Where are we going? I can't go anywhere, I'm not even dressed."

"For what I got in mind, honey, you don't need to be dressed!"

"Gator!" She laughed. "Tell me where we're going."

He grinned and shook his head. "You know, we've got to do something about your hearing." He pushed his face into hers until his lips were just a breath away. "I just told you where we're going. We're going to get married," he said carefully, giving her robe a playful tug upward. "Cause if we don't, I'm afraid I might do something—"

"Married?" she repeated, her eyes wide. He was back to being overbearing again, but she didn't care, she loved it.

"Now don't tell me you're going to start fussing again?"

"Me? Fuss?" She tried not to grin. "I'm not the one who is always fussing. You're the one that—" His mouth stopped her words. Her body responded immediately. Tremors of delight skipped up and down her frame as she tightened her arms around him. Sighing with happiness, Victoria rested her face contentedly against the warmth of his shoulder as he crossed the room.

"Wait!" She stiffened and tried to climb down from his arms but he held her tight.

"Now what?" he bellowed, glaring down at her and coming to a sudden halt.

"I can't get married in a robe!" She grinned wickedly. "Think of what the pictures would look like! And what about James? I have to tell him. I want him there."

"James already knows. He's waiting downstairs in the car."

"Gator McCallister!" She thumped his chest. "You had this all planned!"

Gator just smiled and brushed his lips across hers. Victoria tightened her arms around him, not worrying about whether the robe was where it was supposed to be. *She* was where she was supposed to be, and that was all that mattered.

He pulled his lips free and moaned. "Tori, honey, if we don't get married real quick, I'm afraid we're going to have the wedding night before the wedding. Now, I'm going to walk past that closet over there, and the first thing your hand lands on you grab. Got it? That's what you're going to wear. One chance is all you get. Now, are you ready?"

Victoria laughed and nodded. Someday, she had a feeling, this was going to make a very interesting story to tell their children. Their children. She sighed in contentment.

He walked past the closet and she tried to get him to slow down, but he paid no attention. She grabbed the first garment her fingers landed on and pulled it loose.

Gator stopped abruptly. His eyes popped when she held up the white gauze dress that bared her shoulders. Laughing, he swung her up higher in his arms and stomped through the doorway. "Prissy lady!" he bellowed. "Let's go get married!"

# *Epilogue*

Trailing her hand absently through the thick mass of hair across Gator's chest, Victoria chuckled softly.

"What?" Gator asked sleepily, tightening his arm around her. "What's so funny?"

Her throaty laugh filtered through the darkness of the room. "Now I know why they call you a legend."

"Victoria!" Gator playfully plucked her fingers from his chest and adjusted himself more comfortably against her. "That's not exactly why. But I guess it'll do for now." He sighed deeply. "You getting hungry?"

"Hungry?" she purred, letting her fingers slide from his chest to his stomach. He wiggled.

"For food, woman!" He slapped her hand away. "If we don't come out of this room pretty soon, James is going to think we've died."

"Gator, it's only been two days," she purred. "And this is Las Vegas. I'm sure James can find something to occupy his time.'' She sighed wistfully. ''Besides, I told him to go buy me some clothes, since you refused to let me bring anything with me.'' Smiling, she ran her foot up his calf until he squirmed again.

''I told you, where we were going you didn't need clothes.'' He turned his head and grinned at her. She lifted a hand and stroked his chin.

''Gator?'' Her voice was thready and she felt him tense against her. There was still one piece of unfinished business between them. She wanted to get it out in the open now. She needed to clear the air between them.

''You've got a problem? We've been married two days and already that tone of voice tells me I'm in hot water.'' He lifted his head and looked at her carefully.

''I want to tell you something.'' She hesitated, then slid her fingers across his stomach. ''I want you to know why I wouldn't sell you the Cannons.''

Gator groaned softly and tried to pluck her fingers free, but she refused to let go of him. She wanted, needed to touch him, particularly now. ''You're going to start that again? I thought we settled all that back at the house.''

She smiled at him, letting her fingers tease his skin. ''I said I wouldn't sell you the Cannons—''

''Tori, honey, we've already been through—''

''I couldn't sell you the team,'' she said slowly, watching his face, ''because I wanted to give it to you. For a wedding present.''

He frowned. ''What?''

Laughing softly, Victoria pushed her face into his. ''You got a problem? I said, I want to give them to you, as a wedding present.''

"I don't understand, honey." His brows creased in confusion and she lifted her fingers to trace the frown.

"I'm giving you the team as a wedding present. Everyone should give something in a marriage. All I have is the team, and my love for you. They're both yours, forever."

"Oh, Tori," he groaned, and covered her mouth with his. Clinging to him, Victoria allowed herself to be swept away in a wave of passion.

He pulled his mouth free. "Now, I've got something to tell you."

It was her turn to frown. "What?"

"Now, promise you're not going to get mad?"

Victoria looked at him. She should have recognized that mischievous look and the twinkle in his eyes. "I promise," she said solemnly, crossing her fingers under the covers.

"Well—" He grinned broadly. "Do you remember the day you fired me?"

"I remember."

"And do you remember I told you you couldn't fire me because I had a no-cut contract?"

"Yes. A no-cut contract," she repeated, nodding her head in confusion. "I remember."

His face split into a wide grin. "I lied," he said happily.

"What!" She bolted upright, ignoring the covers that had fallen to her waist.

"I lied," he repeated. "I don't have a no-cut contract."

"Gator McCallister!" Victoria yanked the pillow from under her head and aimed it at him.

"Tori—what are you doing? Victoria!" Gator jumped from the bed and ducked as the pillow went sailing past his head.

"Victoria," he scolded, laughing and trying to duck behind the furniture. "Victoria Louise Fairchild! Ladies," he said, deliberately emphasizing the word, "do not throw pillows. It's not polite."

She scrambled off the bed and chased him around the room, waving another pillow in his direction. "I'll give you polite!" she threatened, trying not to laugh as she tossed the pillow at him.

"Victoria!" He grabbed her around the waist and tackled her to the floor, landing squarely on top of her.

"Gator," she said breathlessly as she wriggled around to fit him more comfortably. "You got just one part wrong."

He frowned. "What part?"

"The name's Tori. Tori McCallister." She lifted her arms and wound them around his neck, then deliberately frowned.

"Do you have another problem?" he asked, and she nodded solemnly.

"Let's hear it." He sighed heavily and she tingled as his chest moved against her.

"Well," she said coyly, trying not to smile, "I think I forgot why they call you a legend. Would you care to remind me?"

Gator scooped her off the floor, strode to the bed and settled her comfortably. "Lady," he whispered, letting his lips find hers. "Anytime. Anytime at all."

# COMING NEXT MONTH

**IT TAKES A THIEF—Rita Rainville**
When Dani Clayton broke into the wrong office at the wrong casino, she was caught—by devastating Rafe Sutherland. Dani was determined to get to the right place; Rafe was determined to keep her out. Two such strong-willed people just *had* to fall in love.

**A PEARL BEYOND PRICE—Lucy Gordon**
Not even the barriers from their pasts could prevent the sparks that flew between Renato and Lynette. Renato was a hard man—would he ever understand the pricelessness of Lynette's love?

**IN HOT PURSUIT—Pepper Adams**
Secret Service Agent J. P. Tucker had been trailing Maggie Ryan for weeks. But it wasn't until after he'd rescued her from kidnappers and counterfeiters, and was chased all over the state, that he realized there was more to shy Maggie than met the eye!

**HIGH RIDER—Olivia Ferrell**
Rodeo clown Rama Daniels wanted a stable home life, and she was sure she couldn't have one with Barc Lawson. Barc was a rodeo rider, a nomad. Though he professed he was ready to settle down, Rama knew rodeo was in his blood. Could he ever convince her otherwise?

**HEARTS ON FIRE—Brenda Trent**
Glenna Johnson had always wanted to be a firefighter, and now she had her chance. She knew she could put out the fires, but could she handle the burning glances of station captain Reid Shelden?

**THE LEOPARD TREE—Valerie Parv**
Her first UFO! Tanith had always wanted to see one, and now she had. But was the mysterious, compelling stranger who arrived with it alien or human? Evidence said alien, but her heart said he was very much a man.

---

## AVAILABLE THIS MONTH:

**LOGAN'S WOMAN**
Glenda Sands

**TOMORROW'S DAWN**
Frances Lloyd

**LADY AND THE LEGEND**
Sharon De Vita

**BENEATH A SUMMER MOON**
Juli Greene

**KISSING GAMES**
Pamela Toth

**STRANGE ENCHANTMENT**
Annette Broadrick